TRIPLET
Code

B. B. JORDAN

BERKLEY PRIME CRIME, NEW YORK

This is a work of fiction. Names, characters, places, and incidents either are the product of the author's imagination or are used fictitiously, and any resemblance to actual persons, living or dead, business establishments, events, or locales is entirely coincidental.

TRIPLET CODE

A Berkley Prime Crime Book / published by arrangement with the author

PRINTING HISTORY
Berkley Prime Crime edition / April 2001

The Penguin Putnam Inc. World Wide Web site address is
http://www.penguinputnam.com

ISBN: 0-425-17920-6

To the memory of Thomas E. Kreis, Ph.D.,
1952–1998

Acknowledgments

I greatly appreciate that my friends and colleagues have been a valuable and enthusiastic source of technical advice and inspiration for this book. I would like to thank Hajime Toguchi and Masaaki Odomi for their generous hospitality in Shikoku and Dominique and Raoul Charron for the same in Vendée. I am grateful to Hélène Coppin for legitimizing my characters' spoken French and to Caroline Bikini for information on deep dives in the Pacific and for technical corrections to my manuscript. Mac's research was inspired by similar findings reported in the scientific literature by Ronald Bontrop, whose encouragement is always appreciated. The work of Celeste and Ivan is an amalgamation of published findings from many laboratories investigating mechanisms of virus subversion of the immune system, and the hypothetical data illustrated in chapter 3 were compiled by Lewis Lanier, as his first work of fiction.

With ongoing gratitude, I thank my faithful team of alliterative and nonalliterative supporters. Cynthia Cannell continues to brim with much-appreciated advice and enthusiasm. Natalee Rosenstein, a patient editor, also contributed invaluable suggestions regarding plot design. My writing mentors Jon A. Jackson and Michael D. Lemonick continue to provide inspiration by example.

And, as always, Peter Parham has been supportive above and beyond the call of duty.

Finally, a word about the dedication. Thomas E. Kreis, Ph.D., was one of the six scientists we lost in the airline tragedy of 1998. He was a good friend, as well as scientific colleague, with whom Gillian Griffiths and I exchanged favorite mystery novels. I wish that he could have read the sequels to *Principal Investigation*.

TRIPLET
Code

PROLOGUE

George Churchill could barely hear the guide's voice over the chopper engine. "Say what?" he shouted into the cold noisy air, feeling his words evaporate.

"Brass monkeys weather out there," repeated the guide. His breath steamed out between curled, gloved fingers cupped into a makeshift megaphone.

Churchill had heard the expression before. Cold enough to freeze the balls off a brass monkey. Maybe. But, it wasn't cold enough to freeze the balls off George Churchill. He'd been waiting for this opportunity to showcase his powder skiing technique and he felt grand. He had the perfect audience. Yesterday, at the conference, he had wowed them with his scientific success. It was tremendously gratifying to affirm that he'd been able to second-guess and surpass the goals of most of his colleagues. This morning they would see that he was equally superior on the slopes.

It pleased Churchill that the dishy Norwegian girl from Larsen's laboratory would see his prowess. It pleased him even more that Larsen himself was present, and with his Swedish wife in tow. Larsen, who somehow managed to surround himself with Scandinavian babes, was always bragging about how he shared their skiing heritage. But today Churchill would show him what it meant to be an expert. Too bad that slug Pogue had declined to join them. It was well known, however, that without the enticement of gourmet food, Pogue wouldn't socialize with other scientists.

The chopper veered precariously and angled toward a snowy plateau. The passengers and ski guide hugged their skis and poles between their knees and steadied the metallic bundles with gloved and mittened hands. Having spent most of the previous evening tuning skis and getting the adjustments perfect for deep powder, no one was about to let go of them and risk being disqualified from the excursion for safety reasons.

Then, with sudden calmness, the chopper leveled and gracefully dropped from the sky onto a flat outcropping of rock at the edge of a snowy slope.

"Say hello to powder heaven," said the guide, in his New Zealand twang, breaking the welcome silence after the chopper blades wound down. "I'll push out ahead of you lot, so you can follow me. Then, you drop in the order we planned last night."

Churchill watched the guide sail out into the snow and watched the Norwegian girl follow him. They skied in tandem down the slope about fifty yards, leaving a spume of powder behind them. The girl wasn't at all bad. If Churchill's wife hadn't decided at the last minute to come to the conference with him and if she hadn't been such good friends with Larsen's wife, he probably would have tried to get the

Norwegian girl into bed. A little flattery from someone with his status in the scientific world was quite
effective for seduction. The thought of his easy con-
quests empowered him. Mentally he recited his familiar mantra of clichés. At fifty-five, he was fit as a
fiddle and at the top of the heap. The world was his
oyster.

Exhilarated, Churchill readied himself. A pristine
field of snow was spread out in front of him. The
shifting powder had already swallowed up the tracks
of the two ahead of him. Churchill stepped into his
bindings, heard them click, and crouched down. Then
he put his full weight on his arms and swung his legs
into the door space. He sat on the edge for a moment
to adjust his goggles, before he picked up the poles.
With everything in position, he shoved himself out of
the chopper and angled his skis for contact with the
snow.

What happened next was eventually the subject of
much speculation. Instead of a firm landing on the
packed snow under the powder layer, Churchill found
himself hurtling headlong in what felt like a free fall
through a thick frosty cloud. Having once lost a pole
in powder, he knew that items could slide for great
distances in the nebulous layer between the snowpack
and powder surface. The initial speed of the slide was
exciting and Churchill confidently conjured up the
necessary moves to right himself with panache. After
all, he was much more dense than a ski pole and
resistance should be slowing him down. But then, as
he communicated the information to his legs to gain
control of his skis, he comprehended with horror that

only one of his boots was attached to a ski. The other ski had detached on impact.

The switch to panic was instantaneous. Churchill's nostrils filled with powder. Powder so cold that breathing it was painful. He moved his arms in a swimming motion, attempting to bring himself to the surface to take a clear breath. Then suddenly, the choking sensation stopped. In fact everything for George Churchill stopped. He met a tree. Though he was in the prime of his life, the tree was the superior being.

1

Tenuous Tenure

Celeste Braun recrossed her legs, waiting for the woman behind the desk to finish perusing the fat curriculum vitae that summarized Celeste's career to date. To pass the time, Celeste looked around the familiar office and mentally tallied the decorating changes that had been made since Dr. Rosenthal relinquished the department chairmanship in January. Dr. Dorothy Grantham, known as "Dot" to her associates, had what Celeste thought of as corporate taste. The office was now a place for cutting deals, no longer the comfortable refuge where Celeste and Rosenthal had chatted easily about science and life. Celeste noted that Dot's corporate taste extended to her personal appearance. Her hair, which was probably gray in reality, was artificially straw colored. It was cut into a businesslike bob with bangs, making her age indeterminate between fifty and sixty. The tailored maroon dress underneath the white physician's jacket was equally businesslike. The jacket itself was an intentional holdover from the clinical department that Dot had left in order to become chair of Microbiology. The appointment of a clinician to chair a basic science department at Bay Area University was the result of recent political struggle in the BAU administration.

"Well, Celeste," said Dot, removing her reading glasses and settling them on the chain around her neck. "On balance, I see no reason to delay your tenure review. We all know that the research side of your work started off with a bang in your first few years. Of course, we'll need letters of support from the leaders in your field to verify that your standing is still high. Another paper in a high-profile journal also wouldn't hurt. It's been two years since any of your work was published in one of the top three." Dot paused to recapture her reading glasses and adjust them back on her nose, leafing to another page of Celeste's résumé. It was predictable, Celeste thought, for someone from the clinical side to count as most important the number of papers appearing in the so-called high-impact journals, without considering their content.

"My only real concern," continued the chair, "regards your committee service for the university. I would have expected more participation. We all need to do our part to run this place."

Celeste couldn't deny that the level of her committee service was atypical. Dr. Rosenthal had respected Celeste's scientific reputation and, with uncommon courtesy, protected her from being assigned to too much committee work. This was no mean feat at a university where women were asked to serve on committees five times as often as men, as a smaller number were available to fill unrealistic quotas. This rampant reverse discrimination was having a serious toll on the time commitments of the female faculty members and Celeste was fortunate to have been spared. She couldn't very well explain this to Dr. Grantham, whose local standing was entirely due to her desire to wield power on committees. Furthermore, Grantham was unused to dealing with other female faculty, who were scarce on the clinical side.

Instead, Celeste found herself capitulating. "Do you have any suggestions?" she asked, with as much respect as she could muster.

"Now that you mention it," said Dot readily, "I've been trying to decide who should be assigned as our departmental representative to the committee for the Hidden Point project. I think you'd be perfect." Celeste watched Dot's color-coordinated maroon lipstick stretch into an insincere smile. "The whole challenge with Hidden Point will be to figure out how to split the science enterprise on campus into the very basic, represented by the model systems, and the more clinically related. You're an ideal member for the planning committee, since you have a foot in both camps."

Celeste's heart sank, as it did every time Hidden Point was mentioned. In the sixties, the BAU campus had signed an agreement with the local neighborhood that it would not expand beyond a fixed square footage. That limit was reached in Celeste's third year at BAU and it became clear that the local neighborhood would not give an inch. The result was that the movers and shakers on campus had put their heads together and after a couple of years of deliberation had come up with the Hidden Point project as the magic

solution. The idea was that a new offshoot campus
would be developed on the outcropping in San Francisco Bay called Hidden Point, now a deserted waste-
land of abandoned docks. This region of the city
would welcome the development and BAU would invite selected biotechnology companies to build on
sites adjacent to the new campus buildings to establish closer academic-industrial ties and make it attractive for these companies to invest in the
neighborhood.

The complication lay in the fact that the main
hospital for BAU would still be located at Olympus
Heights. Many of the faculty, even those engaged in
basic research, needed to be near clinics either as
consultants or to have access to patient material.
Deciding who would go to Hidden Point and who
would stay at Olympus Heights had turned into a
logistical nightmare. For Celeste there was an ironic
twist to the situation. There was no question that the
campus atmosphere would change when half the
faculty moved to Hidden Point. Thus, whether she
got tenure at BAU or had to look for another job
elsewhere, Celeste knew that her working environment would be different within a couple of years.
Celeste's work had flourished in the mixed clinical–
basic science environment at BAU. This made it
even more galling to have to agree to serve on the
Hidden Point committee and contribute to the dis-
solution of that synergy.

"I suppose you're right," replied Celeste. "I will be
a typical casualty of splitting the research community,
so I might as well opt for participating in damage
control."

She noted that Dot Grantham's penciled eyebrows raised disapprovingly. "Of course," continued Celeste, with a concession to the party line, "I realize that the campus has no choice and must split, if it wants to grow." Celeste decided to keep to herself her private opinion that bigger was not necessarily better and changed the subject.

"Can we return to the tenure issue?" Celeste asked Dot. "I was wondering if you'd like me to provide a list of potential referees. Of course, I realize that you'll ask others as well—"

"Yes," said Dot, cutting her off. "A list would be particularly useful since one of the main referees I had in mind, Churchill, is now dead. Rather awkward for you, I imagine."

"There's no question that Churchill was one of the prominent members of our field. He had the reputation of being an expert skier too. Nobody can understand what happened. I heard from a friend who was at the conference that the ski guide had personally checked all the bindings and settings and insists the accident wasn't mechanical."

"Well, even experts sometime make errors," said Dot. "I wonder what Churchill's letter would have been like."

"Supportive, I imagine," said Celeste. "Though we did scoop him on the virus assembly pathway story last year, I think he had respect for our work."

"Actually," said Dot, "you should probably have been at that conference. At this stage in your career, you should be out and about, promoting your work."

"Well, I'm off to a U.S.-Japan virology meeting

next week and I've got two more conferences to attend in the next three months, so I thought I could comfortably miss the ski meeting. They're not my favorite meetings, since most people are more anxious to get out on the slopes than to interact with each other."

"Just make sure your visibility stays high," said Dot. "I can't support a nonentity for tenure. By the way, I'll assume that Pogue and Larsen will be on your referee list, so let's hope nothing happens to them."

Celeste didn't think this was amusing, so she answered straight. "Larsen is undoubtedly a better skier than Churchill was and Pogue wouldn't do anything that didn't involve food and wine, so I imagine you can count on them. They ought to have a perspective similar to Churchill's, since both have been scooped at one time or another by work coming out of my lab. Of course, that's only when they got close to what we work on. They could handle it, since they run huge operations and have loads of other projects. I think you'll get a fair appraisal if you ask them."

"I wouldn't want to be anything but fair," said Dot, rising from her desk.

Celeste rose also, relieved the meeting was over. She needed to get back to the lab to fire up her students and fellows. They would be the ones to produce the data for a "high-impact" manuscript.

"Shut the door after you, please, Celeste," said Dot. Her tone was that of a parent who has finished talking to a child and needs to get on with adult business.

Someone should teach this arrogant puppy a lesson

or two, Dot thought to herself. The junior clinical faculty she was accustomed to knew their places and showed Dot the kind of respect she deserved. But then, they were invariably male.

2

Bathing Beauties

The U.S.-Japan meetings on biomedical topics are sponsored by both governments and are held annually at academic conference facilities, alternating between the two countries. Celeste was pleased to have been invited to speak at the virology conference, which was in Japan this year. She had heard that the Japanese hosts always managed to supplement their meager budget with industrial donations, so attending one of these conferences at a Japanese site was considerably more pleasant than attending the alternating conference in the United States. However, the mood was likely to be somber this year. It was the first conference since the ski meeting where Churchill had died. A memorial service was organized for the second evening.

Premature death was not a stranger to the scientific community. Already, during Celeste's career, two of her colleagues had died in plane crashes and one in a motorcycle accident. Scientists were once considered retiring social misfits, but their careers now resembled a cheap version of life in the fast lane.

Increased pressure to obtain research funding was generating a proliferation of conferences, which were intense venues for competition and self-promotion. The travel schedule of a successful and even of an aspiring scientist had become brutal. It had consequently been a shock, but no surprise, to the community when six scientists were lost in the tragic 1998 Swiss Air plane crash. The fact that scientific investigation is to some extent a bid for immortality meant that the scientific legacy of these crash victims was a constant sad reminder of the community's personal losses. Celeste wondered how Churchill would be remembered. In his case, it would be fortunate that his work would outlast the impact of his personality.

Celeste got off the train at Zushi Station, near the end of the Yokosuka commuter line from Tokyo Station. Only the final leg of the trip to the Kanto International Study Center remained. It was early evening and the commuters surged from the train, carrying her along, up the stairs and over the tracks to the station exit, where local buses waited in a semicircle to take them home. Celeste easily located bus number 19, destined for the Kanto Center.

Standing in the queue to pay her three hundred yen to board the bus, Celeste realized that this was the first trip to Japan during which she had to find her own way from the plane to her destination. Her previous trips had been hosted lavishly by Fukuda Pharmaceuticals, for whom she was an occasional consultant. Judging from the meticulous directions to the conference center that the participants had received, it was clear that the characteristic Japanese hospitality was no different in the academic world.

The bus wound its way to the conference center, which was located near the historical town of Kamakura, on a small peninsula south of Tokyo. Celeste tried to keep from dozing. But the trip and time change were catching up with her. Each time she jerked awake, she looked out on a rough, purple sea dotted with surfers in wet suits. The bus seemed to be hugging the coast, in preference to cresting the steep hills that rose to Celeste's left. The conference center was reputed to have a view of Mount Fuji, across the inlet from these hills.

Celeste arrived after the welcome reception and buffet dinner were finished. It was already dark, so the view of Mount Fuji would have to wait. Only one man got off the bus with Celeste, a Japanese participant she didn't recognize, so Celeste presumed that most of the other conference participants had already checked in. Indeed, the check-in desk at the far end of the large glass-enclosed lobby was clear. And when Celeste's check-in formalities were completed, the girl at the desk handed her a note from the participant she most looked forward to seeing.

During her work for Fukuda Pharmaceuticals, Celeste had become good friends with two of the scientists there. One was the virologist Kazuko Hagai, the author of the note. The other was the vice president in charge of all of Fukuda's research operations, Toshimi Matsumoto. Kazuko was head of Fukuda's virus research unit, based in Sapporo, on the northern Japanese island of Hokkaido. Toshimi was located at the Fukuda headquarters in Osaka and was due to retire within the next year. He wasn't attending this conference, but Celeste would see him in two months' time, at another conference in Japan that he was organizing.

Meanwhile, it was a treat to be able to spend time with Kazuko. It would be an understatement to say that their friendship had developed in difficult circumstances. They met shortly before Kazuko's husband was murdered. Celeste had been asked to consult for Fukuda about the scientific circumstances leading to his murder and ultimately to the murder of the previous head of the virus research unit. Celeste and Kazuko had last seen each other in the autumn, at the height of their involvement in another criminal case, when they narrowly escaped the Taiwanese mafia and recouped at a spa in Japan.

Kazuko's note informed Celeste that the women's bathing hours were from ten to midnight and that she intended to be in the public bath after the conference reception was over. She hoped Celeste would join her. Celeste smiled. A hot shower and soak would be perfect before crawling into bed. Having ascertained the location of the baths from the clerk, Celeste went quickly to her room and switched her travel-soiled clothes for the clean *yukata,* a cotton robe, laid out on the bed. She found hotel slippers in the closet and, with her toilet kit in hand, went to meet Kazuko.

By now Celeste was familiar with the communal bathing habits of Japan. Frequently the baths in hotel rooms were only for refreshing oneself. Thorough cleaning was done in "public" baths. In some establishments these could be quite elaborate and there were permanent facilities for women and men. In the less salubrious guest houses, the hours were rotated between the sexes. Celeste knew the drill. She took off her robe and left it in a basket in the dressing room inside the entrance with her toilet kit. Taking her shampoo with her, she passed through a pair of swinging doors and picked up a small wooden bucket and stool in the shower room, which was lined with faucets and handheld showerheads at foot, waist, and shoulder level. Here, Celeste found dispensers for Shiseido shampoo, hair conditioner, and body soap, so her shampoo was superfluous. Celeste washed her body and hair thoroughly, sitting on the stool and rinsing herself with bucketloads of hot water. Now she was ready to enjoy the soaking tubs. Leaving her stool, bucket, and shampoo at one of the washing stations, Celeste opened the glass doors from the shower room into a hot steamy room. There were about a dozen naked women in the room. Celeste recognized Kazuko instantly by the way in which her long black hair was looped up on her head. She was sitting in a large, sunken wooden tub, chatting to two other women. Only their shoulders emerged from the dark steaming water. Celeste approached the side of the tub.

"Celeste," said Kazuko with delight. "So happy to see you." She reached up her hand and gave Celeste's hand a squeeze. "I think you know Janet Pogue," said Kazuko, nodding to a tanned woman with her hair pulled back tautly in a ponytail. "And this is Kirsten Larsen."

"Hi, Janet, nice to see you again," said Celeste, slipping gently into the tub. The heat embraced her. "Ooh, that feels wonderful." Celeste directed her gaze to the other woman, who looked familiar. "Kirsten, I think we've met before, at a conference two years ago in Crete."

"Yes," said Kirsten. "I remember you." Her accent was faintly Scandinavian but her appearance was full-blown Viking. As she spoke, she lifted herself out of the water onto the edge of the bath to cool off. Her pale skin was boiled pink and substantial breasts hung down almost to where her belly bulged under the crease at her waist. Kazuko and Janet popped out of the bath at the same time and made quite a contrast with Kirsten's voluptuousness. Kazuko had a slim girlish body and Janet, who Celeste knew was a serious athlete, had a tough sinewy look.

Janet was the lab manager for her husband, Richard Pogue. In addition to respecting Janet's scientific capabilities, Celeste also respected the fact that she managed to keep fit, though married to a gourmand. Celeste had met Janet frequently at meetings over the years, but realized she had never seen her nude and was shocked to observe that one of her breasts was slashed by a scar where the nipple should have been. She tried not to look at it.

Celeste judged Janet and Kirsten to be in their early to mid fifties. Janet's hair was definitely graying and Kirsten's blond locks were likely touched up. They were both still attractive women. Celeste hoped that in fifteen years or so, she would be as attractive. At the age of thirty-seven, a few well-placed "sun streaks" still concealed what little gray had appeared in Celeste's brown hair. Though her body was not ageless like Kazuko's, her small Renaissance-type breasts were unlikely to sag much. It was her pear-shaped hips she would have to keep in check.

"We were talking about Shelley Churchill, when you joined us," said Kazuko. "She arrives tomorrow for the memorial. I was asking Janet if Shelley is having difficulty."

"You know, we're like the shadow cabinet in England," said Janet. "Shelley, Kirsten, and myself being the wives of Churchill, Larsen, and Pogue. Shelley's the first one to make it to freedom. I wouldn't worry about her."

Celeste found herself shocked by Janet for the second time that evening. This time by her matter-of-fact attitude toward Churchill's death. But, Celeste rationalized, if she thought about it, this attitude was entirely understandable. Everyone in the field recognized that Churchill had been greedy and ruthless and wouldn't be missed. It wasn't surprising that his wife wouldn't miss him either. Celeste also realized that the other wives of her older colleagues justifiably felt their share of oppression and some envy of release from that oppression. Celeste just hadn't considered it before. They were of a generation in which the husbands built their careers on wives who stayed home, cared for the children, and, most importantly, cared for the husbands. All the wives seemed to gain from their husbands being at the top of their profession was to accompany them to meetings in exotic places, a debatable compensation. Janet had even had the humiliation of sacrificing her independence as a scientist. She had become a housewife after finishing her Ph.D. and the only way she could reenter the profession after her children were grown was to join her husband's laboratory. Though it was informally acknowledged that Pogue's scientific success owed much to Janet's insight, he was still the one who was acclaimed by the field.

It seemed that Janet was reading Celeste's mind. "Don't be shocked," said Janet. "It's just that when you get to be our age, you earn the right to tell it like it is."

They were interrupted by the arrival of a younger woman with her preteen daughter. "Hi," said the woman. "I'm Amy Cook, Jim Cook's wife, and this is Tiffany."

Celeste mentally corrected her misapprehension. Maybe it wasn't only the older generation of male scientists that was serviced by their wives.

They all introduced themselves and began to chat about the trips in Japan they planned around the meeting. Amy told them that she, Tiffany, Jim, and their six-year-old son had been in Tokyo for a week already.

Suddenly, Tiffany said to Janet Pogue, "What happened to your nipple?"

"I had cancer, dear," said Janet, not in the least embarrassed. She'd raised children of her own and was accustomed to their curiosity. "But I'm all better now. I was lucky to have caught it early."

"You were," said Tiffany's mother, her eyes wide.

"I had a hell of a time convincing my doctor, though. I was only forty-two, which is rather young for breast cancer, so he wouldn't believe me that I felt a lump in my breast. In the end, I had to go to a public clinic at the hospital to get a mammogram to prove my point. I was fortunate that lumpectomy was the accepted procedure at the time. Lumpectomy, radiation, and chemotherapy did the trick. I've been clean as a whistle ever since."

"Thank God for that," said Kirsten, laying a hand on Janet's arm.

"Well, I think it's Tiffany's bedtime," said Amy, unsure of what other revelations might be in store for her inquisitive daughter. "Nice to have met you all."

"I'm done in, too," said Celeste. "I've got to give my talk tomorrow. And so do you, Kazuko."

"Well, you scientists should get your rest," said Kirsten. "The shadow cabinet can keep playing."

Celeste and Kazuko showered again and moved out to the dressing room to dry off.

"Celeste, I think I should tell you that I saw Mac in the lobby when I was checking in," said Kazuko, when she was sure they were out of range of being overheard.

Celeste could hardly believe it. "What?"

"Yes, Mac. He was in your lab the summer I spent there. John Macmillan is his real name."

"I know his name," said Celeste. Did Kazuko realize the extent of her involvement with Mac that summer? It had happened while she and Kazuko were getting to know each other, so she certainly hadn't discussed it. In fact, their relationships with men played no role in their friendship. For Celeste, it was a relief from her incessantly doomed affairs not to discuss them. And she assumed that Kazuko had not become involved with anyone since her husband's death, but then, she had never asked.

"Will you be glad to see him?" asked Kazuko.

She must know, thought Celeste. Her instincts are too good. "I'm not sure," she answered honestly. The affair with Mac had been a wonderful fling, but hadn't stood the test of distance when Mac started graduate school on the other side of the country. They had split up almost a year earlier and had been completely out of touch. He'd made incredible progress in less than two years of graduate research, if he was already presenting data at this meeting. However, rationalized Celeste, entering graduate school at the age of 45 meant Mac had always been quite focused about his goals.

"Mac says he is taking the place of his boss, who could not come, suddenly."

"Well, it's a good opportunity for him," said Celeste.

Kazuko responded to her ambivalence. "Perhaps he will not recognize you. I almost didn't. But I like the short hair. It suits you."

"Thanks, Kazuko." She didn't need to say more. Her short-haired self, with its familiar long nose, stared back at her from the mirror, wondering what Mac would think. The haircut had been a reaction to the disastrous termination of her most recent relationship, almost three months earlier, on New Year's Day. With it she'd turned over a new leaf, resolving to avoid casual involvements with men. She felt her scars thickening.

Celeste was grateful for Kazuko's warning. She did not want to run into Mac before she gave her presentation at the conference, and it was easy to justify skipping breakfast. Breakfasts in Japan could be challenging when battling jet lag, although a conference center might offer Western options. It usually took

Celeste a few days to stomach the thought of miso
soup and rice with pickles as a substitute for scram-
bled eggs. Thus she was content with green tea from
the tea maker in her room and sweet rice wafers from
the tea tray, supplemented by an apple she had saved
from the airplane, as an accompaniment to reviewing
her slides for her talk.

The schedule that Celeste had received at registration indicated she had half an hour, actually twenty-
five minutes plus question time, to present her
progress of the past year. It was the first time she had
talked about this work in public and therefore she
needed to refresh her memory as to the order in which
she would present the data. By the time she had completed the meeting circuit this spring, she would know
the talk cold, unless she had new data to add.

Celeste timed her arrival at the conference hall,
which was on the top floor of the building, to coincide
with the beginning of the first talk. Mac's boss, the
head of AIDS vaccine development at the National
Institutes of Health, was scheduled to give the second
talk and Celeste was scheduled for the fourth talk,
just before the coffee break. The whole session was
entitled "Virus–Immune System Interactions." A desk
set up outside the conference hall had empty slide
holders, each with a speaker's name taped to the side.
Celeste quickly loaded her slides, checked them on
the test projector, and handed them to the young man
behind the desk, who would deliver them to the projectionist. In Celeste's experience Japanese meetings
were always well staffed with helpful assistants to
make sure things ran smoothly. By the time she entered the conference hall from the back, the lights

were already down and the meeting organizer was finishing his introductory remarks.

Celeste found an aisle seat on the outside aisle, not far from the front of the lecture hall, so it wouldn't take her too long to get to the podium when it was time to speak. She thought she could distinguish the back of Mac's head in the front row, where she expected him, an eager novice speaker. It looked like he was sitting next to Kazuko. She wondered if they had discussed her apparent absence.

Celeste usually had to concentrate hard on the talks that preceded hers. Often they were on topics related to what she was planning to discuss. So she had to be sure that she didn't miss anything that needed comment or that would seem superfluous if she repeated it. Concentration in this situation was difficult at the best of times, since she had never managed to shed completely a palpable degree of stage fright and was usually rehearsing mentally. This morning, concentration seemed impossible. The entire first talk was almost completed and Celeste found she had to read the abstract in the meeting program to get the point the speaker had been making. Fortunately, he didn't seem to be touching on subjects that she would be addressing. All she had been thinking about was the last time she had seen Mac and how disenchanted they both were when things didn't work out. It was going to be impossible to avoid him, so she would have to be civil. And then she heard his name.

"Our next speaker is John Macmillan from Nick Russo's lab. Unfortunately Dr. Russo was unable to come at the last minute, so we are grateful to John for making the trip. He will be speaking on 'Immune

Protection for HIV from Conserved Sequences.' "

Mac rose from his seat, walked over to the podium, and fumbled a bit attaching the microphone to his collar. Celeste held her breath. He looked good. She had met Mac when he was a landscape gardener and part-time student, finishing a bachelor's degree he had postponed for many years after returning from service in Vietnam. Though he was eight years her senior, he had never appeared "grown-up" to her until now. Gone were the faded blue jeans and T-shirt of his gardening days. He was a handsome man and the standard male scientist uniform of khaki trousers and button-down shirt made him look appealingly serious. Celeste could imagine female graduate students throwing themselves at him and felt an inappropriate pang of possessiveness.

Mac looked the audience over leisurely before he spoke. He didn't seem particularly nervous and gave the entire room one of his boyish grins, which, Celeste felt sure, was guaranteed to melt everyone into being receptive to what he had to say.

"I realize that it's totally out of line," began Mac, "that the first time a graduate student's data are presented, it is the student himself who presents them. I have no doubt that Nick would have done a much better job, and I'm sorry he couldn't be here. But we're so excited about the implications of what we've discovered together that I was willing to brave the fire to tell you about it. I'm particularly pleased that one of my former professors, Dr. Braun, is here, so she can see what resulted from her rigorous training." With another charming smile, Mac looked straight over to where Celeste was sitting. Celeste was thank-

ful that it was dark, so no one could see that she
blushed from her toes as she nodded her head to ac-
knowledge Mac's statement.

This time Celeste had no trouble paying attention
to the speaker, though her thoughts were incongru-
ously punctuated by recollections of him in bed,
which she tried to banish. The work Mac described
was indeed exciting. They had been studying why
chimpanzees are far more resistant to HIV infection
than humans are. For these apes, HIV causes only
mild disease. Mac had discovered that the chimpan-
zee's immune system has a preference for reacting
against features of the virus that generally don't mutate, so the chimpanzees can sustain an immune attack
on the virus. This contrasts with the well-known situation for humans, whose immune system tends to
react to parts of the virus that mutate rapidly, allowing
the virus to escape the immune response generated
against it. Mac had prepared a vaccine from DNA that
encoded the so-called conserved features of the virus
and had shown that it could protect chimpanzees from
infection. It seemed quite possible that humans might
also be protected by injection of similar segments of
HIV DNA.

The discussion after Mac's talk was lively and Celeste was impressed with his handling of the ensuing
questions. The disappointed lover in her was temporarily replaced by the proud teacher, a convenient
substitution that made her own presentation easier.

Celeste also had novel data to report. The frequent
mutation of a virus is one way for it to escape an
immune response against it. Celeste described a second strategy in which a virus actively sabotages the

development of an immune response. In her case, she was studying cytomegalovirus, a virus known as CMV, which causes an opportunistic infection in HIV patients but is tolerated as a mild infection in individuals with an active immune system.

While Celeste was speaking, she looked at her audience from time to time, when she wasn't pointing out a detail on the data slides that accompanied her talk. Every time she looked out she noted Mac's attentive expression and was reminded of when he had been a student in her class at BAU. She had been stimulated by his attentiveness then. He had seemed to evaluate what she was saying rather than unquestioningly swallowing it, unlike his fellow students. Now he was only one of many listeners with critical minds. Celeste was therefore relieved when the questions from the audience revealed that the work had been well received.

After Celeste's talk, the audience dispersed for a coffee break. As often happens, individuals from the audience approached the speakers at the front of the hall with more detailed questions to ask privately. Celeste and Mac, as well as the other two speakers in the session, were instantly surrounded by little knots of inquiring colleagues. Celeste wasn't focusing on what she was being asked. She was contemplating the most appropriate way to greet an ex-student, who was also secretly an ex-lover. Then she realized, with a sense of liberation, that it didn't matter. She quickly glanced at Mac, who was intently answering questions, and understood that he had no hold over her. Their personal relationship had been tested and had not survived. Surely she couldn't have been thinking that there was anything to pursue further. Her apprehension about seeing him was attributable to nervousness regarding her talk. With that hurdle successfully behind her, she could be a gracious former mentor and greet Mac comfortably.

Mac was freed first and joined the group around Celeste, which had dwindled to two. Celeste could feel his presence as she patiently answered questions. Finally, the last two interrogators left and Celeste and Mac stood face-to-face. She held out her hand to shake his in greeting, looking at him to read his attitude toward her. He smiled broadly.

"I won't eat you," he said and leaned forward to kiss her cheek. As he did so, under his breath, he said, "At least not at the moment."

Celeste might have melted, if she could have taken him seriously. "Don't be fresh, Mac. You're carried away by your first success."

"Aren't you glad to see me?"

She couldn't lie. "Very. And glad to see you doing so well."

"Thanks," said Mac. "Your respect means a lot to me."

Celeste had forgotten how earnest Mac was. It never failed to disarm her. But she was about to be protected by an unusual savior. She saw Richard Pogue bearing down on them from the back of the lecture hall. He moved more quickly than would be expected for someone of his bulk.

"Celeste," he shouted. "Excellent talk. And you, too," he added to Mac as he approached. "Don't know if monkeys are a good model for humans, though."

Before Mac could correct him and tell him that

chimpanzees were not monkeys but were, like humans, apes, Pogue continued, addressing Celeste. "Hear you're up for tenure now. Just got the letter from your new chair. Didn't know that Rosenthal retired." Pogue spoke in truncated sentences. He was a busy man and didn't seem to have time for extra words, except when they were on menus. Celeste figured that Pogue's wife, Janet, did most of the communicating with the graduate students in the laboratory.

Pogue continued, without waiting for Celeste to comment. "Wonder what Rank'll think about your CMV data. Saw him at the ski meeting. Said he's getting into the same area." It was characteristic of Pogue to mention the ski meeting where Churchill had died, with no reference to the tragedy.

"I think Rank will be pleased to hear about my data," said Celeste. "I worked in his lab when I was an undergraduate and consider him one of my mentors. It was because of him that I became a virologist. I'm surprised to hear, though, that he's moving away from his mutation studies and into this new direction." Celeste realized that she had unintentionally left Ivan Rank off the list of her tenure referees. She supposed he hadn't come to mind because his work wasn't so trendy at the moment. But he'd undoubtedly be someone whom her chair would ask for a letter.

"It's that new fellow they hired at his place. Influence of fresh blood."

"Well," said Celeste, "I look forward to hearing about what Rank is doing. I think he's chairing a session at the next meeting in Japan, since his name was on the abstract committee."

"We're out of that area ourselves," announced Pogue. "Wouldn't want to come up against your lab again." His joking did not disguise irritation. "Anyway, good luck with the promotion." He turned as abruptly as he had butted in and hustled out of the conference hall.

"What was that all about?" asked Mac.

"I'm not sure," said Celeste. "Some kind of power game, I guess."

"I'd think you'll have no trouble at all with tenure," said Mac. "Shall we get some coffee?"

"Good idea."

As they headed up the aisle toward the back of the auditorium, Mac reached out and ruffled Celeste's short hair.

"Makes you look too young to be a tenured professor," he teased. "But cute."

The informal caress was a friendly concession to their past intimacy. However, Celeste wasn't feeling as confident about her promotion as Mac apparently did and the gesture irked her.

3

Abstract Apoplexy

Dot Grantham walked down the corridor from the provost's office to the elevators, her high heels clicking furiously. The meeting had not gone well. She had accepted the chair of Microbiology with the understanding that she would be head of the premier academic department on the Olympus Heights site, when the other basic science departments left for Hidden Point. Being the leader of the elite would be tantamount to being queen of Olympus. Now it seemed that the human genetics program was considering remaining at the Olympus site, too, and was making a bid for some of the expansion space that Dot had her eye on. Not surprisingly, the provost liked the idea that intellectual expertise might equalize at the two sites of his splitting campus. For this reason, Dot was worried that he would encourage the human geneticists to stay by giving in to all their demands.

The only solution would be to step up her recruitment efforts to entice Nick Russo to move from the NIH. If the recruitment looked promising, the provost would have to commit some of the space that human genetics wanted. Dot knew that Russo was tempted. There was likely to be a change of government in Washington, which often meant a change in the appointments at the NIH. Russo had mentioned that he would be particularly interested in moving to BAU if he could have a couple of junior faculty appointments to fill, in addition to resources for his own lab. Dot was jealously guarding the one open junior position in the department for this purpose. She had an idea about how a second one might be freed up. In fact, after her recent discussion with Celeste Braun, Dot felt quite optimistic that she would be able to meet Russo's demands. It had certainly seemed like it might be difficult to find supportive letters for Braun's promotion.

Celeste left for the lab late that morning. She enjoyed working at home after breakfast, surveying the San Francisco skyline. Her diligent search for a condominium with a view had unquestionably been worth the effort. Vistas influenced her mood dramatically. It could even be genetic. Her grandfather had been fond of hiking in New Hampshire, where the low tree line in the White Mountains made spectacular panoramas easily accessible. The view of the Golden Gate Bridge from Celeste's department office, as well as the view of the Pacific Ocean from her own office, had often boosted her spirits in otherwise frustrating situations. Access to these views was almost sufficient compensation for the fact that her laboratory would stay at Olympus Heights after the campus split. If she got tenure, that is.

Looking out from the large dining room table, which doubled as an eating surface and a work surface, Celeste was reminded of the view of Mount Fuji that she, Kazuko, and Mac had recently been treated to. At breakfast, on the last morning of the conference at the Kanto Center, the clouds had finally lifted and Mount Fuji had appeared, suspended like a large conical hat on the horizon. By that time, Celeste was comfortably eating pickles with rice and soup first thing in the morning. She was also comfortably joking around with Mac. She was quite amazed at how easy this was without being involved with him. Okay, there was the faintest hint of sexual tension between them, but they were enjoying each other's neutral company too much to let it affect them. They hadn't had any time alone together at the meeting and hadn't sought it. There was something soothing about being collegial. For the two of them, almost healing. Celeste had developed this kind of relationship with other men, including her long-time buddy Harry. But with Harry, it had never been a question of once being in love. They had always just been friends, who occasionally slept together. His comfortable position as science editor for the *New York Times* also precluded any changes in this arrangement, keeping Celeste and Harry at a convenient distance. Celeste's musings raised a curious question. Had she actually been in love with Mac? More likely it had been an infatuation. Anyway, Celeste had found a novel stability in the lack of romance in her life and was relieved that it was not threatened. She hadn't even tried to probe Mac to find out if he was involved with someone else, an omission that astonished her.

Celeste made herself focus on the day's work. She had only been back from Japan for two weeks and needed to make a list of things to complete before leaving for the next meeting, in two weeks' time. Some of her senior colleagues were chronically on the travel circuit and, for them, being in the lab was a restful break from their peregrinations. Celeste was still at the stage where she found this type of schedule dizzying and her desire to be involved with what was going on in the lab outweighed her desire to escape it.

Celeste's "to do" list came easily and seemed dauntingly long. One of the things she had to accomplish was to write up and send off an abstract for the talk she intended to give later in the spring, at the meeting that Fukuda was sponsoring on the island of Shikoku. She hadn't forgotten Richard Pogue's intimation that she might be competing with her undergraduate mentor Ivan Rank and that he was moderating the meeting session in which she was scheduled to speak. She wasn't quite sure how to handle the situation since she had no firm indication of what Rank was actually working on.

Mac had attended the now infamous ski meeting and had heard Rank speak, the day before Churchill died. Celeste had asked him about it while they were in Japan. Mac recalled that Rank had given his usual lecture about virus variation and escape from the immune response. At Celeste's request, Mac had, upon his return, faxed her a copy of Rank's abstract from the program book of the ski meeting. The abstract had revealed nothing about Rank starting a project that might conflict with Celeste's current work. One thing

Celeste felt confident about was that whether he was working on the same thing or not, Rank would be very excited about the principle of what she was doing, since it was a new angle on virus evasion of the immune system.

Celeste realized that it would be prudent to check with her graduate student who was working on the project to find out where things stood, before she typed up the abstract. So she collected the papers spread across the dining room table into a leather satchel that served as her briefcase and headed downstairs to her car.

Celeste shared her building with a couple who owned a jazz club in the Castro. They occupied the one-and-a-half-story condominium on the ground floor, which extended down the hill one level and opened out to the garden behind the building. When Celeste opened the door to the garage from the small front courtyard, two miniature dachshunds raced out, yapping, between her legs.

"Stanley! Dexter!" Celeste greeted the animals. They were namesakes of the great saxophonists Stan Getz and Dexter Gordon. As she bent down to fondle the dogs, their owner's shaggy head and heavy beard appeared through the opening in the garage floor, coming up from the garden.

"Hi, Celeste," he said with one of his characteristic mournful sighs, which Celeste often thought sounded like jazz riffs. "I hope they're not bothering you. Every day they seem to be more bouncy. Maria and I are thinking we'll have to move out soon to give them more space to play."

"Are you serious, Geoff?" asked Celeste.

"Well, the club's doing well, so we don't have to be here every weekend. We could move out to the water, maybe Half Moon Bay or Stinson Beach— somewhere where Stan and Dex could run on the beach."

"I'd be very sorry to see you go."

"Well, maybe you wouldn't have to have new neighbors. You could buy our place and put them back together. I'm sure it was once all one house."

"I'd love that, but, even if I could scrape the money together, I don't know if my job here will last."

"Tenure review?"

"You got it."

"Well, we haven't put the place on the market yet and probably won't for a couple of months, at least."

Celeste was sorely tempted. She loved the property. Expanding into the lower floor along with the garden level would set her up for life. She'd never want to move. "Please tell me before you do anything."

"Don't worry, you'll be the first to know."

"Thanks, Geoff. I appreciate it." Celeste pressed the garage door button. The door rose with shudder, exposing Celeste's 1978 MGB to daylight.

It was a short drive over the Seventeenth Street hill from Celeste's condominium to Olympus Heights. By the time she reached the lab, Celeste decided that the best course of action regarding Rank would be to write as complete an abstract as possible and then submit the work for publication as soon as possible, preferably around the time of the meeting. She hoped that Karen would have enough data by now to facilitate this decision. Given that Rank had always supported Celeste, she assumed that if they really were competing, they could come to some agreement about submitting their papers for simultaneous publication.

As soon as she arrived at the laboratory, Celeste looked for Karen, whose thesis project centered on the virus immune evasion work. She found her standing in front of her lab bench, holding a piece of X-ray film up to the ceiling light and squinting at it.

"Karen," began Celeste and Karen jumped visibly. "Sorry, I didn't mean to startle you."

"It's okay. I'm jittery from worrying about these experiments. I've been trying to repeat that result I showed you before you left for Japan. I'm pretty sure I'm getting the same effect, but it's not as dramatic. See, here are the infected samples and the amount of surface MHC molecules and here are the uninfected cells. There's apparently more MHC on the uninfected cells. So it seems this virus gene product is causing the MHC molecules to disappear."

Celeste was somewhat reassured. The MHC molecules, formally known as molecules of the major histocompatibility complex, are carrier molecules expressed on the surface of all cells. They display pieces of all the proteins that are present inside cells and thereby show the immune system whether there are any abnormal proteins present, like ones that might be encoded by an infecting virus. If the virus could cause MHC molecules to disappear, the cell's warning system would be inactivated and the virus could escape from recognition by the immune system. What concerned Celeste was that it wasn't clear from Karen's data whether the particular virus gene product she was testing could make all the MHC molecules disappear, which it would have to do to be effective for complete evasion of the immune response.

"I see the problem," said Celeste. "It may be that the virus gene causes complete disappearance of the MHC molecules. But perhaps your infection efficiency isn't very good, so that not all the cells have acquired the virus gene you think is responsible for the disappearance. If you're measuring surface molecules on the whole population of cells and some have none, but others have normal amounts, the average effect will be partial reduction. Couldn't you use a fluorescence-activated cell sorter to look at individual cells?"

"How?" Karen was a student in the genetics Ph.D. program. They had not been taught the various applications of the cell sorter, a machine used primarily by immunologists.

"The cell sorter measures levels of molecules on the surface of individual cells using fluorescent antibodies that bind to the molecules. There are certainly such antibodies available to measure MHC molecules. Then if you want to know which cells are infected, you can add another fluorescent marker that will appear when the virus gene is acquired by the cell through infection. You get a dot plot showing which cells are fluorescent with the MHC marker versus which ones are fluorescent with the virus gene. If your virus gene makes MHC molecules disappear from the cell surface, the two fluorescent populations won't overlap." Celeste drew a hypothetical cell sorter analysis on a piece of paper lying on Karen's lab bench.

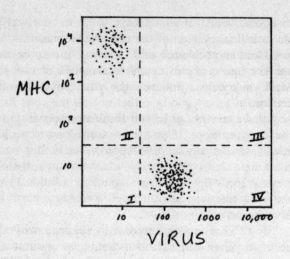

The fluorescence-activated cell sorter measures two fluorescent signals, one from detection of MHC molecules and the other from detection of virus inside cells. Each dot represents the fluorescence measurements from an individual cell and the two signals detected on that cell are each plotted on a separate axis. The plot of the data is divided into quadrants. The data demonstrate that virus infection of individual cells makes their MHC molecules disappear. There are no cells in quadrant I (no MHC signal, no virus signal) because all cells have either MHC molecules or virus. There are no cells in quadrant III (signals from both MHC and virus) because no cells can have MHC when they are infected with virus. The cells in quadrant II have signals from MHC molecules because they have no virus and the cells in quadrant IV all have a signal indicating they are infected with virus and therefore have no MHC molecules that can be detected. The fluorescent signal outputs are in units of fluorescence, on a log scale.

"Cool," said Karen. "That's got to be the way to do it. It'll take me a few days to get the materials I'll need and another week or so to clone the fluorescent marker into the virus gene. Meanwhile, I can still work on trying to improve the efficiency of the infection."

Celeste considered herself fortunate if one in ten of the students who joined her lab turned out to be like Karen. It was working with responsive students like this that made the whole enterprise worthwhile. "Where does that leave us regarding an abstract for the next meeting though?" asked Celeste, partly of herself and partly of Karen.

"Well, I'm convinced you've explained why I'm seeing a partial effect. So I'm willing to commit myself to saying I've identified the gene responsible," said Karen.

"I don't know," said Celeste. "I think we're better off just describing the effect and saying that we are in the process of identifying the gene. That way, if we're wrong, we don't look foolish and if we're right we're not giving it away prematurely. Hopefully, we can write it up soon, though. I heard at the meeting that Rank might be working on similar things, though the rumor hasn't been confirmed."

"He doesn't work on this problem," said Karen. "He's been stuck on virus variation for years."

Karen was referring to the fact that Rank had been the first to characterize how virus variation was responsible for their evasion of the immune response and had worked on the problem ever since. This discovery had established one of the defining principles of the field of viral immunology. Celeste respected him for making a career of working out the details, but students only saw excitement in new concepts. "You never know what he might have moved into," said Celeste. "The nice thing about science is that you can keep doing it but it's never the same and it always leads you in new directions."

Ivan Rank felt his blood pressure rise dangerously when he received the abstract from Celeste's laboratory a few days later. For him, these new research directions were turning out to have a distinctly nasty side. He stormed to the office next door. Wally Dyer would know what to do. After all, it was Wally who had encouraged Rank to switch gears at this late stage in his career.

Ivan Rank was small, rotund man. The fact that he had a full head of wavy black hair at the age of sixty, when most of his colleagues were graying or balding was his chief vanity. That, and his status as founder of the field of viral immunology. He had a whiny voice and when he gave lectures, he consciously lowered it an octave. He didn't have to think about it with Wally and when he began to speak his voice was shrill.

"That bitch!" he began, almost shrieking. "And to think that I trained her as an undergraduate."

Wally Dyer looked at his visitor with solicitous alarm. Rank was bright red. He could blow a gasket any second.

"What is it, Ivan?" asked Wally, as soothingly as possible.

"She must know we're working on this and she has the gall to send me this abstract. For *my* session, no less."

"Ivan, I'm not sure what you're talking about," said Wally. "Surely, you're not going to be threatened by some woman."

"It's not just any woman. It's Celeste Braun I'm talking about. She's working on MHC downregulation by cytomegalovirus."

"No shit," said Wally, forgetting his respectful attitude toward Rank. "She has no originality."

"You can say that again. She knows we've hired you. Any idiot would realize that with your expertise in CMV, you and I would start working on how CMV evades the immune response."

"Ivan, I don't know how to say this. But, being someone who defined the field, you're not used to competition. In the trenches, it happens all the time."

"I agreed to work on this with you, but I never agreed to descend to the trenches. What happened to respect for mentors?"

"I really don't know," said Wally, fueling Rank's fire. "I would never do anything like that."

"No, I know you wouldn't, Wally. That's why it's been such a pleasure having you around. And you're right. I'm not used to the trenches. What do you think I should do?"

Wally was relieved to see that Rank was a shade less crimson. Nonetheless, he spoke gently, in mild reassuring tones. "Well, there's two things, really. First, we can deal with the science. We'll just step it up, so we can be sure that they don't publish first. Since you're chair of the session, you can speak first and make it clear that you've got a paper in press. Look at it like the perfect opportunity to take precedence, in public."

"What's the second thing?"

"That's more up to you," said Wally. "I haven't been in this business as long as you have, but it seems to me that people shouldn't get away with stealing other people's ideas. That's a sort of scientific plagiarism. I would imagine that the higher-ups at BAU wouldn't be too happy to learn that one of their junior faculty had scooped a former mentor by this means."

"You're absolutely right, Wally. This is a matter of scientific justice." They considered themselves scientists of principle. Neither of them subscribed to the more commonly accepted attitude that ideas are cheap and it's the execution that makes them valuable.

Although Dot Grantham was not a bench scientist, she believed in upholding their principles. She was horrified, but thrilled at the same time, when she opened the unsolicited letter from Ivan Rank. In fact, it was quite a coincidence that he had written her, since he was on her list of referees for Celeste Braun's tenure. Now she knew why Celeste had left him off her own list of suggested referees. The words *scientific plagiarism* certainly had a useful ring to them, and Grantham would make sure that they reached influential ears.

4

Napoleonic Nightmare

The high-tech TGV train traveled so smoothly through the apple orchards of Normandy that it was simply impossible for Celeste to stay awake on the trip from Charles de Gaulle Airport to Nantes. Dozing while bypassing beautiful scenery was an unfortunate drawback to these conference trips, which seemed to be falling into an idiosyncratic pattern. At least Celeste would have a second chance to view Normandy from the train, upon her return to Paris from Saint-Malo.

Growing up on the east coast of the United States, Celeste had studied French in public school since the age of nine. At some time during her instruction, she had been struck by two illustrations in a textbook. One showed Breton women wearing elaborate starched lace caps. The other showed a plate of crêpes and gave the recipe for making them, in French. These images had remained with her and instilled a lifelong desire to visit Brittany. Coincidentally, it was the next region north from the Vendée, where the conference was being held. So, Celeste had arranged to stay in the famous Breton city of Saint-Malo for one night after the conference finished.

The Vendée also had an interesting history, which Celeste began to read about as she endured the next idiosyncrasy of her conference pilgrimage. The instructions for reaching the conference site in Vendée were as elaborate, but nowhere near as specific, as the instructions had been for reaching the Kanto Center in Japan. At the train station in Nantes, the participants were expected to find a bus to Fromentine, the town nearest the beach resort where the meeting was being held. Celeste had continued to study French through high school and had even spent five weeks on a summer exchange program in Marseilles, so her French was at least still serviceable for simple tasks like asking directions. The man behind the bus ticket window informed Celeste that she had an hour and a half to wait. She bought herself a *sandwich au jambon* and a bottle of Badoit mineral water and settled down on an outdoor bench near the bus depot to read her guidebook and eat her picnic.

It was the third week in April and the sunshine was pleasantly warm, while the air temperature was perfect for being comfortable in the long-sleeved T-shirt, tweed jacket, and loose trousers that Celeste favored as a travel outfit. She had just finished reading about how Vendée was a refuge for the last royalists during the French revolution, and was about to start reading about the Napoleonic era in Vendée, when a woman spoke her name.

Celeste looked up to see Janet Pogue standing in front of her. "We'll have to stop meeting like this," said Janet, with a terse smile. She sounded almost serious.

"Where's the rest of the shadow cabinet?" asked Celeste, looking around.

"Kirsten's over there, being bored to death by Dick and Lars. They're trying to talk science with Claude Foucault from Nantes. He met us at the train station. And, uh, Shelley Churchill's not here. She will be at the next conference in Japan, though. The one that Toshimi from Fukuda's organizing. That site is supposed to be a real treat, and three of us are going to Tahiti afterward. Toshimi was so kind and wrote to Shelley that she was still welcome at the conference."

Celeste saw Kirsten and the three men standing where Janet had indicated. She closed her guidebook. "I suppose it's time to begin."

Janet gave her a sympathetic look. "I could pretend I didn't see you," she offered.

"It's okay. I'm ready." Celeste put her book away and picked up her luggage, which consisted of a compact garment bag and a cabin bag with wheels.

"Is that all you have?" asked Janet with admiration.

"I have a friend who's a stewardess," explained Celeste. "They take classes in how to pack."

"You'll have to tell me the secret sometime. Now that our youngest finally graduated from college, I expect to be doing more traveling than I used to."

As they approached Kirsten and the others, it became clear that the topic of conversation had moved away from science. "But of course," Claude Foucault was saying, in a heavy accent, "we shall without doubt have the *cuisses de grenouille* from the region." He paused to translate, trying to remember the interpretation used instead of thighs, the literal translation. "The legs of the frog," he explained after a moment. "These frog are special. They were brought from Albania to breed in the regional swamp. We have a lot of swamp in Vendée and much unique food from them."

Celeste observed the group while she and Janet waited for Claude to stop talking. He had his back to them and his attention was fully absorbed by his effort to communicate in English. Richard Pogue, looking disheveled and overweight, stood directly opposite Foucault. He was transfixed by the talk of food. Lars Larsen stood next to Pogue, listening politely, and Kirsten stood next to him. Both the Larsens were tall, and Kirsten was a bit taller than Lars. Larsen, a lean, fair-complexioned man with thinning hair, was of Swedish background, but had been born in Minnesota, where he still lived and taught. He had spent his postdoctoral fellowship in Stockholm for both political and sentimental reasons. There he met and wooed Kirsten, whom he had brought back to Minneapolis with him. Celeste had always found her to be defiantly foreign. But in this situation, adjacent to her husband and wearing a more filled-out version of what Celeste was wearing, Kirsten looked like an all-American woman. In comparison, Claude Foucault looked slim and elegant. He wore impeccably pressed khaki trousers, tasseled shoes, and a white shirt open at the neck with a dark green wool sweater draped over his shoulders like a cloak. His jet black hair was slicked back and when he finally turned around to confront what had captured the attention of his audience, Celeste saw that he was wearing dark, aviator-

style sunglasses. These he immediately removed and
he crinkled his face in a charming smile, producing
lines that suggested his age was somewhere between
Celeste's and the rest of the distinguished company.
Celeste also noted the outline of a blue packet of Gauloise cigarettes in his shirt pocket.

"Ah, Madame Pogue, I see you have found a young
lady for me."

Celeste noted that Janet did not even cringe at being called Madame instead of Doctor. "Yes, Claude,
this is Celeste Braun. Celeste, this is Claude Foucault.
You know everyone else."

"Oh, *pardon,* Dr. Braun. I did not know that Celeste Braun would be so young, and so attractive. It
is truly *un plaisir* to meet you." For a moment, Celeste thought he was going to kiss her hand, but he
shook it instead.

"Charming," said Kirsten, a bit jealously. "Hi, Celeste."

"Nice to meet you, Dr. Foucault. Hello, Kirsten,
Lars, Dick." Celeste nodded at each in turn.

Dick Pogue was impatient with the interruption.
"Claude was just telling us about the regional spe-
cialties. I knew the local oysters and white wines were
outstanding and I'd heard of the *moutons de prés-
salés,* but apparently there are other treats in store for
us." Celeste was amused that Janet had used the word
treat to refer to traveling, while for Dick it had never
lost the childhood meaning of something special to
eat. She wondered how they would survive their
empty-nester life together.

"What are *les moutons de prés salés?*" asked Celeste. "It sounds like salty sheep."

"Exactement!" exclaimed Claude. *"C'est ça.*
These sheep, they live near the sea and eat the grass
which is wet by the sea, so they taste of the sea."

"So what else will be at the banquet?" asked Pogue,
unable to contain himself.

"Did I mention yet the eels? *Les anguilles grillées?*
These are from our famous canal. But of course, *la
pièce de résistance* will be *les pommes de terre de
Noirmoutier."*

"Potatoes?" asked Pogue, skeptically.

"Oh, these are not just any potato," answered
Claude. "These potatoes are grown on the island of
Noirmoutier, where the banquet is being held. They
are a special small potato with a sweet flavor. They
are boiled for a long time in broth, then seasoned with
la fleur de sel."

"Yes, yes," said Pogue. "I know the *fleur de sel.* It
is the best part of the salt produced from evaporation
of the seawater. Antoine brought me some for my
kitchen, last time he visited." Antoine Suchet was
head of the research institute at the hospital in Nantes
where Claude worked.

"You will be able to see Noirmoutier from the resort where we will stay for the conference. It is a very
interesting place. Now there is a bridge to Noirmoutier, but before, it could only be arrived at by *le Pas-
sage du Gois. Et qu'est-ce que c'est Le Gois?* you
may ask. *Le Gois* is a channel traversed by a road
that was built by Napoleon. Actually, they say the
road was built by the slaves of Napoleon. You will
see. It is a beautiful stone road, but dangerous. It is
passable for three hours only at low tide. The tides
here, they are famous. They are fast and go out a long

way. You know *le Mont-Saint-Michel?* It is a monastery in Brittany which is accessible only at low tide. We have the same tide here. Many get trapped by the tide. You will see. *Le Gois* has *refuges* for those who are trapped. But these are only poles to climb, with a small basket for a man to sit. If he is in a car or on a horse, these must be left behind."

Celeste was captivated by Claude's sense of the dramatic. She could imagine the sea washing over an abandoned vehicle, as the driver climbed a *refuge* pole and had to witness the flooding of his only means of transport. She had heard of the tides in the northwest of France, even read stories about them. Apparently the local people lived by the tide tables. There had been plenty of disasters to remind them that timing was everything. "Is it true that every shop has the yearly tide table posted?"

"Absolutely, mademoiselle. We will give the table to all of the conference participants. It is a law."

Celeste supposed she did look like a mademoiselle compared to Janet and Kirsten, and she was on her own, but it seemed a little inappropriate.

"Ah," said Claude. "Here are more of our colleagues." They all looked in the direction of the train station and saw two men approaching. The older man was wearing a light gray suit and muted tie, carrying a leather overnight bag and briefcase. The younger was wearing a corduroy jacket and blue jeans, carrying canvas luggage that looked like duffel bags. The second man was Mac.

The first man spoke as soon as they reached the group. Celeste realized from his greeting that he was Antoine Suchet, Claude's boss from Nantes. "Excellent, Claude. You have found our friends." Then, to all he said, "I am so sorry I could not be here directly to greet you. We had a visit to our institute from a scientific commission sent by INSERM to evaluate our facilities. As you are no doubt aware, INSERM is one of our two government funding agencies for laboratory research in France." He paused to let the importance of his excuse sink in, and then continued. "It is lucky, though, that I am late. I find this young man who is lost, looking for the bus."

"Hello, Mac," said Celeste, taking charge of her sudden delight in seeing him again. "Everyone, this is John Macmillan from Russo's lab. He worked with me when he was an undergraduate. You heard him speak at the Kanto Center."

Once greetings had been exchanged and introductions made, Mac said, "We all must have been on the same train from Charles de Gaulle Airport. I thought my French was okay, but I completely misunderstood the directions to the bus station. If Dr. Suchet hadn't spotted me walking in the opposite direction, I'd probably have missed the bus."

"Well, at least you asked directions," said Kirsten flirtatiously. "Unlike most men I know." She looked pointedly at her husband, who ignored her.

Mac flashed her a dazzling smile. "But I still needed to be rescued." Now it was Celeste's turn to have a jealous twinge. When Mac had been in the gardening business, he had cut quite a swath through the community of bored society matrons whose landscapes he had designed. And Kirsten was an attractive specimen.

"Where's Russo?" asked Larsen, abruptly interrupting Mac and his wife. "He was supposed to be here and at the Kanto Center. What's going on?"

"Nick had really hoped to make it to this meeting, considering he had to miss the last. And it's doubly disruptive for me to come because things just seize up on the project when I'm away. But, the government is going crazy with this surplus at the moment and Nick was called a few days ago to give a deposition in the House, scheduled to start tomorrow. Jane Stanley is pushing really hard to get some of this surplus money diverted to an increase for the NIH budget."

"How is Jane doing?" asked Celeste. Jane Stanley, head of the National Institutes of Health, had been Celeste's doctoral supervisor and they had remained good friends since Celeste left Jane's laboratory. Recently, Celeste had helped to clear Jane's name from a false accusation of scientific fraud. That incident had precipitated Jane's retirement from Harvard and ultimately freed her to accept her current government position when she was vindicated.

"We rarely see Dr. Stanley," answered Mac. "She's mostly stalking the corridors of power. But she came by the lab about two months ago to chat with Nick and it looked like she was thriving."

"Well, I talked to her more recently than that and I certainly got that impression. The mood at the NIH must be so radically different now from what it was when I was reviewing grants a few years ago, when government spending was under such scrutiny. Then, only eleven percent of the grants submitted were being funded. Now it's almost double that and the NIH budget continues to increase. I guess the eradication of the deficit made it possible for the government to realize that increasing the NIH budget was only a drop in the bucket compared to defense spending."

"I don't know," said Larsen, in his flat midwestern whine. "I heard that Russo wasn't that happy at the NIH and was looking to move. It sounds like having too much money is giving him too much responsibility."

"Yeah, I heard that he was considering a move, too," added Pogue. "Isn't it to your place?" he asked Celeste.

"If he is moving to BAU, I haven't heard anything about it. But our new chair runs the department differently than Rosenthal did." Celeste wondered if Grantham was up to something behind her back. Surely if Russo were being offered a job at BAU, Celeste should have been consulted. Their research interests were so complementary.

"Perhaps it's just been discussed among the senior faculty," said Pogue. The remark seemed unnecessarily nasty and Janet rolled her eyes at Celeste.

The conversation was broken by the arrival of their bus. After some fussing, the luggage was stowed in a compartment in the side of the bus and the scientists with their French hosts climbed aboard. Celeste took a seat by the window and Claude, who had followed her onto the bus, asked graciously if he could join her. She was pleasantly surprised to see the disappointment on Mac's face when he saw that the seat next to Celeste was occupied. Kirsten and Janet had seated themselves together behind their husbands, so Mac was stuck with Suchet. He sat right behind Celeste and Claude, where he had to listen to Claude's persistent flirtation throughout the trip.

They rode for an hour through the low, flat countryside. The fields were bordered by drainage ditches, evidence of their tenuous relationship with the sea. Claude leaned closely over Celeste's shoulder as she looked out the window, and eagerly pointed out every detail, including the fact that sheep they saw grazing were *les moutons de prés-salés*. He smelled heavily of Gauloises and a very strong aftershave lotion. Celeste began to feel a little nauseated by the combination and was relieved when the bus reached Fromentine.

Fromentine consisted of picturesque white cottages with red tile roofs and wooden shutters painted either white or sky blue. Between the cottages, Celeste could see water extending behind them. Close to the shore stood wooden structures, like crates on short stilts. Claude explained that these were for oyster cultivation. The water behind the cottages was an effluence from a local river, creating the perfect conditions for oysters.

All the local passengers descended at Fromentine. The bus was apparently making a special trip to take the scientists on to the resort, located a few miles farther, on the Atlantic. Before they set off on this last leg, Kirsten and Janet rearranged their seats to be in front of Celeste and Claude, so that they could benefit from Claude's commentary.

The land between Fromentine and the shore was covered by a sandy pine forest. To Celeste, who was familiar with the scraggly New Jersey pine barrens, the trees' long, silky-looking needles seemed elegantly luxurious. As soon as the bus left the forest, the ocean spread out in front of them. There was a low hump visible on the horizon, which Claude informed his listeners was l'Île de Noirmoutier. He pointed out the thin sliver of a bridge stretching over to the mainland at the south end of the island. Kirsten and Janet wanted to know the name of the bridge, presumably for a private tour they were planning. Evidently they did not want to risk driving through *Le Gois*.

The road crossing *Le Gois*, Claude told them, connected to the middle of the island from a village north of Fromentine. They would be having dinner at that village in the evening and would surely have a view of *Le Gois* from the restaurant.

At last the bus pulled up in front of the resort, a weather-beaten building of white painted wood and glass that looked like it had been built in the fifties. Celeste was thrilled to find her room had an ocean view and she could see a sightseeing boat heading toward the mainland from Noirmoutier. The view wasn't sufficient, however, to refresh her completely. With the knowledge that nothing was expected of her before the opening reception and dinner, she set her alarm clock, stripped off her travel clothes, and, crawling under the crisp white duvet, immediately fell asleep.

Celeste was not disappointed by *Le Gois* when she finally saw it. As Claude had promised, dinner the first evening of the conference was held in a restaurant on the street that led up to *Le Gois*. The road crossing *Le Gois* was under water when the tour bus carrying the scientists arrived at the restaurant, but they were informed that the tide was on its way out and that the road would be visible after dinner. *Le Gois* was about three miles across and punctuated by five *refuges.* On the way into the restaurant Celeste could see the platforms of the *refuges,* sticking up above the water, marking where the road extended under the sea.

Dinner started with the most succulent oysters Celeste had ever tasted and looked like it was going to end with *mousse au chocolat.* In between, Celeste could hear Richard Pogue exclaiming about the grilled eels, his comments penetrating through the conversation of her earnest dinner companions. Celeste, anxious to see the road across *Le Gois* without fifty fellow observers, excused herself, as though going to the toilet, and left her mousse untouched.

Outside an almost full moon had risen. Celeste crossed the small street in front of the restaurant and walked over to a slight rise on the other side of the street, which provided a vantage point for viewing where the sea had been. There, snaking toward Noirmoutier, was a ribbonlike mosaic of rough-hewn stones, about a cubic foot each. Stones so heavy that they would have had to have been laid by slave labor. The moonlight glinted off the wet sand adjacent to the road, which itself was raised slightly above sand level. The stones, also still wet, sparkled magically. Now fully exposed, the *refuges* stood like wary sentinels. Celeste could make out pegs on the sides of their poles for climbing up to the platforms.

She sensed someone crossing the street over to where she stood. It was Mac.

"Surprised to find you alone," he said. "Has your companion gone for a cigarette?"

"Oh, Mac," said Celeste. "How can you be snide with this inspiring site in front of you?" She looked at him with disappointment.

"I'm sorry." His genuine chagrin was conveyed in the look he returned to Celeste. "I've been trying hard to behave correctly."

"I know you have," she replied, her tone softened. "And I appreciate it. It's been good to get reacquainted like this."

"I think so too," said Mac and he looked at Celeste again. But she was fixated by *Le Gois.*

Mac stood quietly by her side, taking in the glistening expanse with her. "I've always wanted to see these tides, since I read about them in high school French class, when we learned about the monastery at *le Mont-Saint-Michel.* I even booked a night in Saint-Malo at the end of the meeting to see them, because I didn't realize the tides extended this far south."

"That's amazing," said Celeste. "I'm going to Saint-Malo, too. Also inspired by my French lessons. We might as well travel up there together."

"I daresay there will be others making the same trip," said Mac. "I'll ask around."

"I don't particularly want to explore in a group," said Celeste. "But you can, if you want to."

"You have a point. Anyway, it could be nice—"

What Mac had planned to say was truncated by the exodus of the rest of the group from the restaurant. Claude, holding a lighted cigarette, immediately sought out Celeste, and Mac backed off.

• • •

The following morning, Celeste gave her talk, without much time for preparation. Traveling in the opposite direction from Japan meant that it was difficult to wake up in the morning. Celeste counted on the fact that she had already given the talk once to get her through. Once again she was scheduled to follow Mac. He, too, gave the same talk. As is often the case, it was useful to see the data again and listen again to the interpretation. Outsiders might wonder how scientists could stand being on a circuit where they heard each other's talks more than once, but multiple exposures to the same data were helpful in trying to grasp the significance.

For the scientist, it was also useful that while the speaker list did not change substantially, the audience changed almost completely from meeting to meeting. These nonspeaking participants generally presented their data on large posters that were mounted for viewing during separate "poster sessions." The data were often preliminary, but frequently quite interesting, and Celeste enjoyed circulating and talking with the poster presenters. Many were the heads of small laboratories or were students in large laboratories. Celeste often recruited such students to join her laboratory as fellows upon completion of his or her degree. The poster sessions were ideal opportunities to evaluate how a student worked and, more importantly, how that student felt and thought about the work.

A change in audience also meant a change in questions to answer after a talk. Celeste became aware of a blond man, about her age or perhaps a bit younger, sitting next to Pogue in the front row, making remarks to Pogue throughout her talk. When he was not talking to Pogue, he was nervously playing with the edges of his mustache. She wasn't surprised when he raised his hand to ask a question when she had finished.

"I couldn't help but notice that the experiment showing a reduction in MHC was done with cloned viral DNA and not with whole virus. This suggests you must have some idea of which virus gene is responsible for the effect. Would you be willing to share that with us?"

Celeste was surprised at his acumen. It was a question that was likely to be of interest primarily to someone working in the area. She had meant to ask Karen to change the title on the slide, so that she wouldn't have to hedge. Now she wished she had followed through. "We do have some idea, but we're not absolutely sure and I'd hate to make a statement that might later turn out to be incorrect."

As she turned to the audience to answer a few more questions, Celeste saw the blond man whispering furiously to Pogue. She wondered who he was.

She wasn't in suspense for long. When the session was over, Pogue came up to her, bringing the blond man with him. "Celeste, you must know Wally Dyer," he said.

"No, we've actually never met," answered Celeste. Dyer was tall and earnest-looking, resembling a clean-cut young missionary. "But I certainly know your work. It was actually your publications that got us interested in having a look at CMV. I hear you've joined Rank's department. How's he doing?"

Wally Dyer could not very well say that Rank had just suffered a nerve attack, which he attributed to receiving Celeste's abstract. "Oh, he's fine. He's excited about our new directions."

"Oh, are you collaborating?"

"Well, as a matter of fact, together we're investigating the same effect you just reported. I assumed you had heard about it."

Celeste's heart sank. "Not exactly," she said honestly, looking to Pogue for corroboration. "Dick told me about a month ago that you guys might be doing something similar, but I couldn't find any mention of it in recent abstracts or in the literature."

"Well, we've only just made the same breakthrough that you have," said Wally defensively.

"Could try to publish back-to-back papers," said Pogue. "Somehow can't picture Rank thinking he should defer to anyone, though." Pogue enjoyed making frank statements that made people squirm.

"I had actually thought of proposing exactly that, if it turns out we're working on the same gene," said Celeste. "Maybe you could talk to him about it," she suggested to Wally.

"We don't know if you're working on the same gene, since you won't tell us which one you think it is," he replied sullenly.

"But we're just not sure yet. We've narrowed it down to a region of DNA. However, there may be more than one gene there. Which gene are you focusing on?"

"I don't think I can tell you that," said Wally.

"Well, I'll talk to Ivan. He's known me since I was an undergraduate and we've had a good relationship in the past. I'll give him a call when I get home and we can discuss how to proceed."

Wally felt totally helpless against what he perceived as willful ignorance. Thank goodness Pogue had a sympathetic ear. "Fine," he said, in a skeptical tone that suggested he didn't believe Rank would want to talk to her. "Shall we get some coffee, Dick?"

"Sure thing, Wally. See you, Celeste."

Celeste was kicking herself for not looking more carefully at the abstract booklet that she had been given upon arriving at the meeting. But when she sat down and went through it, after picking up her slides from the projectionist, she saw that neither Wally Dyer's nor Rank's name was there. Dyer must have decided to come at the last minute, after the abstract deadline. If she weren't counting on this publication to boost her tenure file, the situation wouldn't matter anywhere near as much. Now she'd have to be diplomatic about suggesting they publish together, so she wouldn't be scooped. Dick Pogue's attitude was also making her nervous. Would he really write the supportive letter that she had anticipated?

The hotel where the meeting was being held was sufficiently old-fashioned that an international phone call had to be booked at the front desk and made from a booth in the lobby. Wally was self-conscious about the public negotiation that accompanied placing a call and could not be as open with Rank as he would have liked, for fear that someone might overhear him. Then he realized that for the sake of Rank's well-being, it was probably a good thing he had to be circumspect until he got home and could ease him through the situation. All he said when Rank finally picked up the phone was, "I've found out where they stand and we're definitely ahead. Also, I had a good chat with Dick Pogue. He's been asked to write a letter of support for her tenure."

"Oh, Wally. What would I do without you," Rank exclaimed with a grateful sigh.

5

Déjà Vu

The heavy hitters gave their talks on the second day of the meeting in Vendée. Celeste observed that neither Janet Pogue nor Kirsten Larsen was present when their husbands spoke. This was understandable in Kirsten's case, as she had no scientific interest. But since Janet was running Pogue's lab, the audience's comments on the work would have meant something to her. Celeste surmised correctly that it was likely Janet had heard it all before, far too many times.

What concerned both Pogue and Larsen, later in the day, was that their wives hadn't shown up for the bus to the banquet. Everyone at the meeting had boarded one of two buses provided by the meeting organizers and one of the buses had already set off. It would be necessary to take the route over the bridge to get to Noirmoutier, since *Le Gois* would not be passable until late in the evening for the return trip home, after a concert in the garden of the restaurant where they were to dine. On top of the pressure to begin the banquet on time to coordinate with the concert and the tide, Pogue was extra anxious that he should not miss a bite. He and Larsen were impatiently pacing the parking lot in front of the hotel, when both wives hurried out.

Celeste was sitting with Claude, near the front of the waiting bus. Or rather, Claude was sitting with her, having once again glued himself to her side. From what Celeste could overhear, the wives had been out all day sightseeing and had simply lost track of the time. Their tardiness hardly merited the furious tirade that Pogue unleashed, which was audible to everyone on the bus.

"Ooh la la!" commented Claude, raising his eyebrows at Celeste and fanning the air with one hand. It was such a stereotypical gesture that Celeste had to stifle a smile. She nonetheless agreed with the sentiment.

The banquet was held in a small château on Noirmoutier that had been turned into a restaurant. It boasted a single Michelin star and was the only restaurant in the region to receive any Michelin rating at all. Aperitifs were served in a terraced garden that faced the mainland. At this time in the evening, only the tops of the *refuges* above *Le Gois* were visible.

The scientists delivered by the first bus were already enjoying glasses of kir made from local wine and stood around the garden, discussing various points that had been raised during the conference. Celeste headed for the table where wine was being served, followed closely by Claude. Somehow he managed to light a cigarette without missing a step. Just as Celeste was beginning to think that she would never be free of him, Janet Pogue walked up to Claude.

"Claude, I was wondering if you could help me out," she said. "I hope you'll excuse me, Celeste."

"No problem at all."

Janet explained her mission. She needed Claude's assistance in communicating with the chef so that their table would be served the local escargots that she had bought that day. Apparently, Antoine Suchet had told Pogue about the escargots and the chef had promised to fix them if they brought them over from the mainland. Janet opened her tote bag and showed them a plastic bag full of snails. Claude and Celeste exchanged glances. They were both impressed that Janet was so devoted to her husband that, even after he had embarrassed her in public, she was still looking after his interests.

"It would be *un plaisir* to assist you, madame," said Claude. And he gallantly held out his arm to escort Janet to the kitchen as her interpreter.

Liberated from Claude's company, Celeste helped herself to a glass of kir. Larsen had made it to the table ahead of her and was already holding forth to a small group around him, which included Mac.

"That was an amazing game," he was saying. "Wasn't it, Chuck? We really whipped their butts."

"Yeah," agreed Chuck, one of the other scientists, who was hanging on Larsen's words. "Who would have thought a team of forty-something scientists could make a group of teenage boys bite the dust."

"See, it was like this, Mac," said Larsen, bursting to retell the story. "At the Gordon conference last year, we challenged the kids who wash the dishes to a game of basketball. They were so sure they could beat a bunch of old guys like us. Well, we had strategy and, actually, were in better shape. They had nothing and we just creamed them. They couldn't believe what had happened to them."

Mac caught Celeste's eye as she eavesdropped on the conversation and raised his eyebrows ever so slightly. She cocked her head to suggest escape. A moment later he mumbled something about not being good enough at basketball to hang out with that crowd and slipped away to join her. They began to walk together toward the edge of the terrace to look out over the sea.

"First of all, they're at least fifty-something, if they're a day," said Celeste. "I don't know who they're trying to fool. Second of all, can you imagine slaughtering a bunch of kids by playing slick basketball and then boasting about it?"

"And when there's so much else to appreciate in this fabulous setting," said Mac. "Let's forget it."

"You're right," said Celeste, taking a deep breath and enjoying the garden. "Oh, look. Lily of the valley, under that bush over there."

She walked over and bent down to smell the flowers. Mac followed her. They caught the attention of Antoine Suchet, who was chatting with some colleagues near the flowers. He came over to Mac, in whom he had developed a fatherly interest.

"I see you have found our *muguets de Nantes.* These flowers are a *spécialité* of my city. All the plants around here, they came from Nantes." He gestured toward the flowers. "They say if you give only one *muguet,* you will never see each other again. If you give three, you will be friends forever. You must give her three," Suchet instructed Mac.

"Oh, no," protested Celeste. "We can't pick the flowers here."

"But of course you can. It is only three and in a good cause, I think," replied Suchet, looking at Mac.

"Don't you want to be friends forever?" asked Mac of Celeste.

"But of course I do," she replied, unconsciously mimicking Suchet.

"Then please take these from me," said Mac and he plucked a bouquet of three and handed it to her.

"Ah, *l'amour,*" teased Suchet.

"L'amitié," corrected Celeste.

"Friendship, too," agreed Mac, smiling.

"You two must sit at our table," said Suchet. "Madame Pogue has arranged an extra course after the oysters. These are local escargots from a farm near Fromentine. She and Madame Larsen made a visit there today."

"I don't know about snails. They make me think of slime," said Mac, as Claude approached them.

"Oh, you must try it," insisted Suchet.

"Your imagination is too strong," chided Celeste.

"I don't need an imagination to think of slime," replied Mac, in a whisper that only Celeste could hear. He did not relish the idea of spending the meal watching Claude slobber over Celeste, but he didn't want to be rude to Suchet.

The atmosphere at the privileged head table was practically ceremonial. Pogue made pronouncements about everything that was served. He treated his fellow diners to a long discourse on the oysters and an even longer discourse on why the wine served was the perfect accompaniment for the oysters. He was so long-winded that Claude, who was sitting next to Celeste, on the opposite side from Mac, had to excuse himself for a cigarette. And Janet Pogue had to get up to use the toilet. So the two of them missed the lecture on the escargots that were about to be served. Finally, the chef brought the snails to the table with a flourish. Each was bubbling appetizingly, in its own little shell. There were six shells on each plate, which fit snugly into the depressions made expressly for serving them. Except for the plate served to Richard Pogue: this had seven snails, a bonus for the connoisseur.

Mac raised his eyebrows at Celeste, across the table. "Rather him than me," he said, in reference to the extra snail.

The snails disappeared quite rapidly and even Mac declared that they were delicious. There was only one more course to go before the *moutons de prés-salés* and the renowned *pommes de terre* from Noirmoutier.

Pogue was just getting into the stride of his next lecture and took a sip of the wine that had been selected to go with the frog legs. Suddenly he spit out the wine, inelegantly spraying the table in front of him.

"Richard!" exclaimed Janet.

"I'm gonna be sick," Pogue said and jumped up from the table.

Janet jumped up too. "I'll take you outside," she said and hurried him out of the dining room, through the front door of the restaurant.

Suchet, looking worried, followed them out.

"I guess he had one snail too many," joked Mac.

A few minutes later, Suchet rushed back into the dining room and announced with distress, "Monsieur Pogue, he is very ill, *très malade. Est-ce qu'il y a un médecin ici?* Is there a *docteur* to assist?"

A few of the assembled scientists were also practicing physicians. As a group they rose from their places and headed for the exit where Suchet stood. Celeste was interested to see that Wally Dyer was among them.

The rest of the diners were dead quiet. They could hear someone groaning loudly, presumably Pogue. Then they heard shouting in French. Celeste could just figure out that they were calling for a car belonging to the restaurant staff and discussing whether *Le Gois* would be passable. Apparently, not yet, since the next discussion was about the quickest route to the bridge and the location of the closest hospital. Then they heard a car pull up at the restaurant door. Its engine idled for a couple of minutes and then it took off, screeching.

The room started buzzing softly, but quieted down immediately when Suchet appeared at the dining room door, with the physicians behind him.

"Richard Pogue is *en route* to the hospital," announced Suchet. "It is not far, so he should be in good hands very soon. Now, please, my colleagues. Finish your excellent dinner. We will enjoy some chamber music afterward, before we return to the hotel by *Le Gois.*"

As Suchet rejoined the head table, Kirsten Larsen stood up to ask him something privately.

"Yes, yes, she is with him," Celeste heard Suchet answer. Evidently Kirsten had asked after Janet. Then

Kirsten absentmindedly sat down in the place vacated by Pogue and started pushing the snail shells around on his plate. It looked like she was playing a solitaire game of Chinese checkers. "I hope Janet's okay," she said, mostly to herself.

The waiter came to the table and began to clear the snail plates, dumping the shells into a pile and stacking the plates on his tray. Just as Kirsten handed him Pogue's plate Wally Dyer came rushing up to the table.

"Stop, stop!" he commanded the waiter, holding up his hand as though he were directing traffic. "We must save the snails. We should check all the food that Pogue ate."

It was too late. As Wally spoke, the waiter had turned the plate over and added Pogue's shells to the growing pile.

"Well, then," said Wally, turning to Suchet, "we should save all the shells."

"I suppose you are right," agreed Suchet with a sigh. "I will make sure of it." And he instructed the astonished waiter to put all the snail shells in a bag.

The following morning, Wally Dyer's prescience was praised by the local police. There had to be some explanation for why Richard Pogue had died on the way to the hospital. With no other clues, they might as well begin by analyzing the food he had eaten, though it was a long shot, since no one else at the table had suffered from food poisoning.

If it was food poisoning, then the cause of Pogue's death was simply bad luck, the only bad luck he had experienced in his sixty years. Had he made it to the hospital in time, they could have pumped his stomach and saved him. But the bridge between Noirmoutier and the mainland had been blocked by a stalled car. Just as the car carrying Pogue was trying to cross, traffic had come to a complete standstill. The tow truck for removing the stalled car had arrived only minutes before. Janet Pogue suffered the nightmarish experience of sitting in a cloud of Gauloise tobacco smoke and watching her husband die.

The scientists were stunned when Suchet made the announcement about Pogue. First Churchill, now Pogue. The giants were falling. There was no question that the field would be different without these strong personalities at the top. Different, and perhaps more friendly.

The conference was scheduled to finish at noon, but Suchet, with his grim news, had terminated the final scientific session before it began. He told the bewildered audience that they were all free to go, except those who had shared the table with the Pogues the previous evening. The local police had some routine questions for them relating to this unfortunate accident. He asked them to please come to the front of the conference hall.

It seemed natural for Celeste and Mac to seek each other out, as the meeting participants silently departed. Mac put his arm around her shoulder and gave it a friendly squeeze. "You okay?" he asked.

"Mmm," replied Celeste. "I didn't like him, but I still feel sad. His presence will be missed, unlike Churchill's."

"I know what you mean," said Mac. "It's good

we're going to Saint-Malo and not straight home. It'll give us a chance to recover."

"I'm glad you're coming with me," she said.

They walked over toward the podium, where the Larsens were speaking with Claude and Suchet. Celeste and Mac stood by while the Larsen's completed what appeared to be a domestic squabble.

"I must join Janet at the hospital," said Kirsten emphatically. "She will need some support. Can you imagine how awful it must be to organize this? Arranging to move the body and everything?"

"But, Kirsty," whined Larsen, "you know our flight back is tonight and I leave for New York in two days. I've got to get back. There are all kinds of things going on that I read about in my e-mail this morning." Larsen never went anywhere without his portable computer, which could be hooked up to the Web. That morning he had been obliged to negotiate with the hotel switchboard operator for the privilege.

"Perhaps I can help," intervened Suchet. "Claude can go with Madame Larsen to the hospital and my assistant will arrange to have her ticket changed. I will make sure that you get back to Paris for your flight tonight. You can be the first to speak to the police, then Madame Larsen, then Claude."

Mac said, "Antoine, this is dreadful. I am so sorry that it has happened in your domain. Would it be all right if Celeste and I packed while the rest of you speak to the police?"

"Yes, of course, Mac. This is a good idea. The police will be seeing people in the small dining room, to the side of where we have the *petit déjeuner.*"

Claude moved around to Celeste's side. "Perhaps I

will not see you later," he said. "*Quel dommage*. I hope that this is *au revoir* and not *adieu*." He grasped Celeste by the shoulders and kissed her three times on alternate cheeks.

"How romantic," said Kirsten to Mac, who silently disagreed. "Nice meeting you, Mac." She held out her hand and when he took it, she leaned forward and kissed him, only once, on the cheek. Then turning to Celeste, she said, "See you at the next conference."

"Bye, Kirsten. Have a good trip back, and please give my condolences to Janet. I'm glad you're going to join her." Celeste then shook hands with Larsen and followed Mac out of the hall.

Meeting the French police was like being imported into a novel by Georges Simenon. The local inspector, Charron, even smoked a pipe during the interrogation. He was accompanied by a younger officer in uniform, with a bristling dark mustache. The inspector's English was as good as that of Suchet and Claude. In his youth, after training at the police college in Nantes, he had spent an unforgettable year on an exchange program with the Detroit police. The younger man did not speak at all during the interview.

"You are the last one," Inspector Charron said to Celeste. Mac had finished packing before her, so had been interviewed first. "Please tell me about the snails."

Celeste recounted that Claude had helped Janet Pogue talk to the chef about preparing the special dish. And that only their table had been served the snails. But no one else was sick. She suggested that Richard Pogue might have eaten something on the sly, in the afternoon, that no one knew about. He did like to eat.

"So I understand," said Charron. "You are not the first to suggest that he might have had a secret snack. It is an interesting theory. It is one that Madame Larsen also suggested. But her husband does not recall that Monsieur Pogue was on his own after the lectures were finished. He believes he was all the time looking at, how do you call them, posters?"

"Well, I did see him while I was at the poster session. But I went up to my room to have a nap and change before the banquet." Indeed, Pogue and Wally Dyer had been inseparable that afternoon and made the rounds of the posters together. It had bothered Celeste enough to notice it.

"Let me ask you one more thing and then I will let you go on your trip to Saint-Malo."

Evidently Mac had revealed their plans. Well, they weren't hiding anything and even if something were going on between them, there would be no need to hide it. After all, they were both unattached. Or were they? Celeste realized she still didn't know Mac's current status.

"Why did your colleague George Churchill die?" Charron interrupted Celeste's reflection with his final question.

"I'm probably the only one you've spoken to who wasn't at the conference where he died," said Celeste. "But it's my understanding that he had a ski accident, doing some expert skiing. Both Pogue and Churchill considered themselves experts in more than science."

"It is interesting that you should see this common character. It seems their special expertise caused them both to die. Do you think that is just coincidence?"

"Of course," said Celeste, perplexed. "It's remarkably unfortunate, but I can't imagine any reason that they would be killed. Yes, there are people who disliked them, but that is normal in our community. Murder is not the usual recourse in that case," continued Celeste, with just a hint of irony.

"Yes, I am familiar with academic behavior," said Charron, with a knowing smile. "Your community is famous for its jealousy." Celeste suddenly realized that a police inspector at home would have taken her remark at face value and she was grateful for Charron's sensitivity.

"May I go now?" asked Celeste.

"You are free, mademoiselle," said Charron, gesturing with his pipe. "By the way, may I recommend the restaurant *Le Pêcheur* on *La Digue* in Saint-Malo? It is located exactly where *La Digue* stops at the beach before the city walls. The *fruits de mer* is *formidables.*"

"Thank you very much, monsieur. I am looking forward to *fruits de mer*. We will try it."

Celeste and Mac arrived at the Saint-Malo station around three in the afternoon. A sharp wind was blowing and the sky was overcast. Looking at the map in Celeste's guidebook, they figured out that both were staying in hotels along *La Digue,* the seawall that extended from the walled city along the north coastline for about two miles. Upon arrival they saw that *La Digue* could have been described as a walkway between all the hotels of Saint-Malo and the sea. The area had been developed in the nineteenth century, along with the elegant promenade which topped

La Digue. The hotel addresses indicated that Mac's hotel was closest to the city. They decided to drop his bags at his hotel and continue in the taxi to Celeste's hotel, from where they would walk back toward the city along *La Digue.*

Mac's hotel was typical of most the tidy three story-buildings lining *La Digue.* Celeste waited in the glassed-in lounge overlooking the sea while Mac checked in.

Celeste's hotel was much more elaborate. It was a functioning spa, patronized for health cures. When they set out on their walk back toward the city, they saw several portly people in French-style athletic gear, facing the wind on a platform extending above the beach and moving their limbs with serious determination. The tide was high, rising rapidly to its peak, and the waves lapped around the platform where the health enthusiasts stood.

Celeste was wearing a sweater under her tweed jacket, but still felt the chill as she and Mac proceeded along *La Digue.* It was refreshing to walk briskly into the wind, which blustered sufficiently that it was difficult to speak to each other. They concentrated on the outline of Saint-Malo ahead of them, steadfast within its walls, resisting the buffeting of the wind and sea.

Celeste was disturbed by the deaths of Pogue and Churchill. They were reminders of the fragility of existence, which made it all the more exhilarating to be enjoying this pilgrimage to Saint-Malo, fulfilling a lifelong fantasy. So many fantasies were never fulfilled. Celeste wondered if Mac was thinking along the same lines when he looked over at her and smiled.

They proceeded steadily toward the city, passing
elderly women wearing woolen overcoats, walking
tiny dogs, similarly attired. As *La Digue* curved with
the coast, a medieval fort atop a small island came
into view. Celeste moved toward the wall at the sea
edge of the promenade to take a look at the fort, using
the birding binoculars she wore around her neck. As
she focused on the fort, a huge wave broke against
the wall, completely soaking her and the binoculars.
Mac stepped back just in time to avoid being doused.

"That'll teach me to spy on a military installation,"
laughed Celeste.

"You're absolutely dripping," said Mac.

"Don't worry. I'll dry off quickly in this wind."
Celeste was more concerned about wiping off her binoculars than about the rest of her.

They continued on for another half mile or so. Celeste did dry off, but at the expense of most of her
body heat. She began to shiver.

"You okay?" asked Mac. Celeste's lips were blue.

"I'm pretty cold," she admitted.

"I think you should get inside. My hotel's not far.
We could have a brandy or something to warm you
up."

"Sounds great," said Celeste.

They were inside the lobby of Mac's hotel within
ten minutes and he ordered two cognacs from the
woman at reception. She brought them the drinks in
the lounge where Celeste had waited earlier. The huge
snifters came with a pitcher of water, but they both
sipped them straight.

Celeste felt the liquor sear down into her guts and
shivered again. Mac reached out his hand and touched

her jacket, then her cheek. One was moist and the other icy.

"You don't feel good," he said. "I suggest a hot bath, immediately."

"You're right, I don't feel so good," confessed Celeste. The situation had taken on a dreamlike quality. She didn't think twice about picking up her cognac and following Mac upstairs.

Mac opened the door and let Celeste in ahead of him, then walked straight into the bathroom and started to draw a bath for her.

As soon as he emerged, he said, "You better get those clothes off." He started rummaging in one of his canvas bags, and pulled out a plaid flannel dressing gown. "Here, put this on. I'll stand at the window."

Celeste was astonished. "Traveling with a bathrobe? I'd never have thought it of you, Mac."

He looked a bit embarrassed. "You only have to go to one Gordon Conference and share a mixed bathroom to invest in one of these. Here, put it on." He retreated to the window and looked out at the sea, while Celeste stripped off.

"I'm decent," she said.

Mac turned around and went back into the bathroom to turn off the water.

"Ready," he said.

Celeste walked in and looked at the steaming water. Then she looked at Mac. She never got into the bath.

His embrace was hungry. Hers equaled it.

"Oh, Celeste," he said, kissing her face and neck and opening the robe and kissing her breasts, belly, and below. "I've thought about this so often. Since we split, there hasn't been anyone like you. I need you."

Celeste melted immediately. She knew she felt the same.

They somehow made it to the bed, Celeste helping Mac shed his clothes en route. "I'll warm you," he said. And he did.

At the moment that he was poised over her, ready to enter, Celeste had an intense feeling of déjà vu. Mac was her man, and he belonged inside her.

6

Flics' Fantasy

"Baker, gimme a pencil, quick," commanded Hy Lockwood, M.D., the chief medical examiner for the state of Utah. He held his hand over the telephone mouthpiece.

The deputy obliged and watched his superior dutifully scribble down a long string of numbers on the back of a pizza delivery menu, and repeat them back to the person on the other end of the line.

"Okay, got it," said Lockwood. "I'll call back as soon as I can." He paused, listening, then said, "You're welcome, I'm sure. Okay, bye."

Lockwood hung up the phone and turned to Baker. "Would you believe it? I just had a guy from France on the phone, an Inspector Sharon. Wanted to know about one of the helicopter ski accidents this winter. Told him I'd call him back. Need to find the file."

"I'll get it," said Baker, since he knew this was Lockwood's way of asking him to. "Which one is it?"

"The victim's name is Churchill. Apparently he was a scientist. I think it's either the one in Snowbird

or the one in Park City. There's a lotta scientific conferences at both places."

"Yup, got it," said Baker, pulling a file from the
overstuffed cabinet. "Churchill was the victim at
Snowbird."

"Give it here," said Lockwood, holding his hand
out, and then, as an afterthought, "please."

"What's he wanna know?" asked Baker.

"Just if there was anything fishy about Churchill's
death. They're following up some theory about a
Unabomber type who's out to get scientists."

"On what basis?"

"Evidently an American scientist died over in his
neck of the woods in France—didn't quite get the
name of where they were. Sounds like the guy died
of food poisoning. Sharon's suspicious 'cause no one
else had any symptoms. And because, get this, 'food
in France is never bad.' But they were eating shellfish,
for heaven's sakes. Anyway, this guy Churchill is in
the same scientific field as the guy who died in
France. So they cook up this theory that since America is full of crazies who attack high-tech types, this
must be a plot. He even had a name for the perp."

"And what was that?"

"Bioblaster, only he pronounced it 'B.O.-blaster.'
I'd say B.O. is about how this theory smells."

"I guess that's what you might expect from police
who are called *les flics.*"

"Why are they called that?"

"Don't know," said Baker. "I just remembered it
from my high school French class. It's slang."

"I hope so," said Lockwood. He leafed through the
thin file on the Churchill accident. "Looks like a

clear-cut case of the usual. Someone who thought he
was a better skier than he was. Seems to have lost a
ski on impact. I guess we still have the file pending
'cause the ski hasn't turned up. Should be closed out
when the snow melts and we find the ski. I'll let
Sharon know he'll have to wait until June to disprove
his theory."

Later the same day, Celeste returned home to San
Francisco. The first thing she saw, getting out of the
shuttle from the airport, was the For Sale sign in front
of her building. She felt betrayed. Then, she was beset
by a flood of more complex feelings. Geoff and Maria
had promised to tell her before they listed the property. But now, what could she do about it, anyway?
It was difficult enough to contemplate bidding on the
property without knowing the status of her promotion.
Mac's reentry into her life only made her dilemma
worse.

Celeste picked up her accumulated mail from the
basket in the garage where her departing neighbors
had left it, and noticed that it contained a note from
them. Then she unlocked the filigreed security gate to
her part of the building and hauled her bags up the
stairs to the second-story entrance to her condominium.

The first thing she did, upon entry, was to walk
over to the window with the view of the city and open
the drapes. Then she opened the envelope from Geoff
and Maria.

At least they were apologetic, and went to great
lengths to explain the situation. The note informed
Celeste that the pet psychiatrist had confirmed that

Stan and Dex were in need of a less confining space to play, and that living in the city was having a negative effect on their sensitive personalities. Geoff and Maria had then spoken with a friend who was a real estate agent and she had told them that in the current runaway sellers' market, they could expect to enjoy two rounds of bidding on their condominium. The agent had advised them to have a month of open houses on Sunday afternoons and to accept the first round of bids the following Friday. They could then offer a counterbid and entertain a second round of bids. It was such a long process, they were sure Celeste would understand why they wanted to get started right away. They would be away until midweek, looking for a place on the coast, and would call Celeste as soon as they returned. The first open house was scheduled for the following Sunday.

Geoff and Maria certainly weren't going to jeopardize any potential profits. So if Celeste intended to bid, she'd have to be competitive. Considering the timing, it sounded like the first bids would be made shortly after Celeste returned from the next meeting in Japan. If a purchase looked at all feasible, it wouldn't do any harm to make a bid in the initial round. It would at least keep her in the running. As if she didn't have enough to worry about, Celeste would now have to look into whether she could mobilize the necessary financing. This wasn't exactly a welcome addition to her anxiety over the developing rivalry with Rank, the concern about her tenure review, and, of course, the disquieting issue of Mac.

Mac was not something that Celeste had counted on, planned on, or even wanted. Yet, the warm reality of Mac seemed to be everything Celeste needed. Previously, she'd dismissed him as just a good lay. A great lay. In fact, the best lover she had ever had and probably would ever have. But this resurgence seemed to be about more than sex. The whole world seemed brilliant and her senses heightened. This state unquestionably had something to do with what had happened between them, which was impossible to analyze rationally. There was no specific moment indicating that some kind of balance had been tipped, but it had definitely tipped.

Celeste dreamily reviewed the time with Mac, as she looked out over the city. After their almost desperate initial lovemaking, they had slept. When they woke, they made love again, taking the time to relish each other. Celeste flushed, thinking about it. Then, amused at their unexpected indifference to Brittany, they finally made the pilgrimage into Saint-Malo and wandered the twisting, cobbled streets in a pleasant daze. On their way back to *La Digue,* they stopped for a meal at the restaurant that Inspector Charron had recommended.

The inspector had been right. The *fruits de mer,* heaps of local shellfish, was spectacular. Replete with succulent, salty flavors and fresh white wine, they had even been able to share the catharsis of joking about Pogue's pretentious lectures over the last shellfish that they had eaten. Mac also confessed that Claude's attentions to Celeste had made him furious with jealousy. Though now, he had decided he could be grateful to Claude for stirring up his true feelings. Perhaps it was this simple honesty that had won Celeste so completely. Spending that night together and their discussions the following day, during the return train journey, about how to arrange their next meeting, seemed destined. As they parted in Charles de Gaulle Airport, each for a different coast of the United States, they knew they would not be separated for long.

Obviously, it was not convenient for someone like Celeste to fall in love. If that was what was happening. As it was, Celeste couldn't have picked a worse time. Her career was unstable and she wanted to buy a house to settle down in San Francisco. She wondered what the pet psychiatrist would have to say about her sense of self-possession.

To Karen, the following morning in the lab, Celeste seemed impressively self-possessed. Celeste's lab personnel were well aware of Celeste's upcoming tenure evaluation. The threat of an imminent scoop by Rank and Dyer was exacerbated by this pressure. Therefore, Karen was pleased to report that she had all the tools in hand to do the cell sorter experiment they had discussed before Celeste left. The control experiments had worked. Individual cells receiving viral DNA were detectable on the machine, so now it was a matter of analyzing these for their levels of MHC molecules. Then it was just a matter of testing different pieces of viral DNA to find the gene responsible for making the MHC molecules disappear.

"If Rank and Dyer really had the gene, they wouldn't have been so anxious to ask you about what we have," Karen pointed out to Celeste. "They can't be any further along than we are."

"I hope you're right," said Celeste. "I want to be

prepared for the meeting next month in Japan, though. They're undoubtedly going to show their hand. Since they've got to piss on the tree, so to speak. You know, claim the territory. Although I've spoken twice in public about the concept, someone with Rank's status will always gain priority. I think we've got no choice but to have the gene by then."

"I'm not making a choice," said Karen. "I will have it. This method you suggested is foolproof."

Celeste wanted to hug her, not just for her cooperative spirit but to absorb some of her youthful confidence. Celeste would need some confidence when she met with Grantham that afternoon. The insistent tone of Grantham's secretary, when she called about setting up the meeting, had not been very reassuring.

Each member of Celeste's research group worked at an assigned bench and desk, effectively representing eight independent research stations for which Celeste was responsible. This meant she had responsibility for funding their research, including their salaries, as well as for setting the research problems and guiding her personnel to solve them. As such, academic laboratories were a classic apprenticeship situation. The compensation for the lab head, known as the principal investigator, or PI, was that until the lab members became independent investigators in their own right, their work was credited to the PI's laboratory. The compensation for the trainees was acquiring the intangible skills needed to do original research.

After she spoke with Karen, it took Celeste an hour or so to make the rounds of the lab, inquiring of the rest of the students and postdoctoral fellows how their projects were going. She then retreated to her office to confront the mail and e-mail that had accumulated in her absence. However, her discussion with Karen had reminded her of the unpleasant conversation with Wally Dyer and it kept resurfacing in her thoughts. Celeste finally came to the conclusion that the best course of action would be to speak with Rank directly.

She had to move several piles of papers to locate the directory of the Federation of American Societies for Experimental Biology, known to its members as FASEB. This book, essentially a phone book for anyone who was anyone in science, was an indispensable tool in this clone-by-phone era. Celeste couldn't help noticing that one of the piles she moved aside was over a year old and had been generated as a byproduct of the second-to-last grant proposal she had submitted. A nearer pile was the residue from the most recent grant submitted. But now was not the moment to tidy up. Celeste found the FASEB book behind the second pile, where it must have slipped after she last used it. Rank's phone number was, of course, listed. Celeste tapped it out.

"Hello, you have reached the telephone of Ivan Rank," said a recorded male voice, and Celeste hung up. Hers was not the sort of issue that could be explained in a voice-mail message. Nor did she want to leave her number for a return call, which might give Rank the upper hand. She needed to catch him unawares, to discuss things in a friendly way.

While she was thinking about when to call Rank again, Celeste's computer performed its hourly check of her e-mail. Reflexively, she responded to the icon

that indicated she had new mail. Expecting more bu-
reaucratic rubbish, Celeste was pleased to see she had
received a message from Harry Freeman at the *New
York Times*. She also received a message from Janet
Pogue.

Celeste first checked what Janet had to say.

Janet was organizing a memorial event for Richard
Pogue, to be held the weekend after next in Montana,
where they lived. The "event," as it were, would con-
sist of scattering Richard's ashes in the Bitterroot
River, near the laboratory where he served as director.
Janet particularly hoped that Celeste would be able to
come. Celeste was, apparently, one of the few women
Pogue had had respect for. So Celeste had been right
after all in thinking that Pogue would have written
her a supportive letter for her promotion. Well, it was
too late now. So the least she could do was attend the
event, and provide some support for Janet, even
though she could ill afford more time away.

Harry's e-mail message was perplexing. He was
writing to ask Celeste if she knew anything about an
item he'd picked up from a French newspaper. The
piece in question mentioned Richard Pogue's death,
which was how it had come to Harry's attention in
the first place. As science editor, he had his assistant
routinely trawling the international papers for articles
relating to science. This article mentioned a police
theory about a plot to destroy biomedical scientists
and pointed out that Pogue was the second scientist
in his field to be struck down recently, in the prime
of his career. The motivation of the hypothetical perpetrator, the so-called bioblaster, was attributed to
growing anti-intellectualism in America.

"Is this for real?" wrote Harry. "If it is, you better watch out!"

Celeste's puzzlement became astonishment as she read through Harry's message. Inspector Charron had asked her to consider a connection between the two deaths, but hadn't seemed particularly convinced of it. Nor had he seemed like a scaremonger. Some French newspaper reporter must have picked up on Churchill's death and elaborated a story to make it more interesting. It was a rather horrible coincidence to lose two leaders in the field within a couple of months. But, as had emerged from Celeste's discussion with the inspector, both men had characteristic vanities that had ultimately been responsible for their deaths. No more connection than that was necessary to understand what had happened. Celeste wrote back to Harry and recounted what she knew. She also wrote, in no uncertain terms, that he would be foolish to publish anything about the bioblaster theory without corroboration.

Celeste began to work her way through the pile of memos on her desk. Three of them were from the heads of Ph.D. degree programs at BAU who were concerned about the effects of dividing their faculty between the Hidden Point and Olympus campuses. She was not grateful to Grantham for appointing her to the Hidden Point oversight committee. Trying to deal with the impact of dividing the scientific programs on campus was like looking at the pathology slides for a cancer patient and finding out the illness was more widespread than anticipated.

It wasn't long before Celeste's stomach told her it was dinnertime in France. She realized she would have to get some lunch to fortify herself before meeting with Grantham. She thought she should try phoning Rank again before she stepped out. Just as she reached for the phone, it rang.

"Celeste," said the voice on the other end slowly, making her name sound like an endearment. It was Mac.

She wondered how his voice could have such a profound effect on her. It invaded her pleasantly.

"When can I see you?"

"Mac, we just saw each other."

"Not enough."

"Well . . ." Celeste mused.

"I'll come out to spend the weekend. How about a week from Friday?"

"You can't. I won't be here. I just told Janet Pogue I'd attend a memorial for Richard, in Montana."

"I'll meet you in Montana, then."

"I suppose you could," said Celeste. "I'm sure Janet wouldn't mind if you were there, as long as there's room."

"Why wouldn't there be room? I'll share your bed, of course. That's the idea."

"They're putting everyone up at the Millstone Wildlife Refuge. It's not very big. I've stayed there before. In fact, it was at the end of the summer you spent in my lab, just after you left for grad school. Pogue hadn't moved there yet."

"Why did he move there anyway? I didn't think that he would ever be able to leave the restaurants of New York."

"Janet told me that during his last couple of years at Rockefeller, there was a lot of internal politics.

Also, or maybe because of it, Pogue developed an ulcer and he had to eat at home more often. She said he was a real pain about eating at home, too. Even worse than he was in restaurants. Anyway, I guess he figured that, if he was eating at home, it didn't matter where home was. Apparently, they're both originally from Montana and they liked the idea of going back. So when the directorship of the lab up there came vacant, it was a perfect opportunity."

"That's an NIH lab, right?"

"Yeah, it has been since the thirties, when the federal government expanded it to bring some employment to the area during the Depression. But it actually started earlier as a state effort to study Rocky Mountain spotted fever. The NIH still supports it as an infectious disease lab, after all these years. It's in a beautiful spot, in the Bitterroot Valley. And the Millstone Refuge is right on the river."

"Sounds fantastic."

"Well, I can't imagine that everyone she's invited will be able to attend, so if I e-mail her right away that I'm bringing someone, it should be fine."

"I guess we'll be out of the closet."

"Were we in the closet?" asked Celeste. It seemed so natural to be attached to Mac.

"Not as far as I'm concerned, if you're not. I can't see that a relationship should pose any problem for your situation at BAU. After all, I'm movable."

"Mac, you're sounding pretty serious."

"I'm feeling pretty serious," he said.

Celeste was too stunned to pursue this further. "I'll let you know what Janet says, okay?"

"Okay," said Mac. "Love you."

"Me, too," said Celeste, instinctively. She could hardly believe it.

Celeste smiled at Dot Grantham when she entered the chair's office. She couldn't help being in a good mood. However, Celeste's greeting did not influence what Dot had to say.

"Celeste, I'll get straight to the point." Celeste noticed that Dot's chartreuse two-piece outfit brought out a matching tinge in her hair. "I've had a pretty damning letter from Ivan Rank, which came while you were away. He more or less accuses you of stealing his ideas."

"What?!" exclaimed Celeste. This couldn't be happening. "There's been a terrible misunderstanding. In fact, I've been trying to get hold of him by phone to find out what's going on. I heard something about this from Wally Dyer, his collaborator, while I was at the meeting."

"I'm not sure I would try to talk to Rank, if I were you," advised Dot. "His perspective seems quite immovable. He was actually considering going to our provost about it, but I dissuaded him. After all, intellectual property in academia is very hard to prove." Celeste noted that Dot did not say that Rank might be wrong, just that his complaint would lack grounding.

"Dot," said Celeste. "I've done absolutely nothing wrong; I've only followed up an interesting scientific problem. Of course I think about similar problems to Rank. After all, he trained me. But, in the world of bench science, ideas are cheap. It's getting them established with data that matters."

"I don't know," said Dot. "As a chairperson, it's impossible to ignore a letter this strong. I'm going to have to keep it in your file. It'll be up to you to make sure your other letters are sufficiently supportive to counteract it. By the way, now that Pogue is dead, you'll have to come up with a substitute."

"Would Janet Pogue, his wife, be okay? She ran his lab and, in fact, indicated that he had talked in favorable terms about me."

"She's probably a research associate or something of the sort, right?"

Celeste nodded concurrence. "But she has a Ph.D."

"No, absolutely not acceptable. You should know that a letter from someone with that kind of appointment isn't going to cut any ice."

"Fine," said Celeste. Then she had an inspiration. "Have you got Nick Russo on your list? I'm quite sure he's familiar with my work and could write a good letter."

Now Dot's face took on just the slightest chartreuse tinge, coordinating with the rest of her outfit. "Yes, I could ask Russo. But you know, he's actually considering taking a job here. I wouldn't want him to think we're trying to push him to accept our existing junior faculty."

Celeste felt sick. Dot Grantham had just tipped her hand. Russo had been offered a job. He probably wanted junior faculty positions to fill. He had probably been promised Celeste's position. And, what made it even worse, Mac was very likely one of the young and promising scientists that Russo would like to bring with him.

Celeste didn't have to ask herself what Dot had to

gain by Russo's joining the department. As part of her committee responsibilities, Celeste had just read the memo from the head of the Human Genetics program, suggesting they might stay at the Olympus site if they could expand into some of the space promised to Microbiology. Russo's hire would not only ensure that Micro kept all of its space but it would undoubtedly bring the department even more resources. This had to be the root of Dot's animosity toward Celeste.

For a preposterous moment, as Celeste considered her dwindling list of supporters, the specter of the phantom bioblaster raised its head. It occurred to Celeste that whatever might motivate such a criminal, the goals seemed to be remarkably in line with those of her own chair—to eliminate any referees who might have been in favor of Celeste's promotion.

7

Dust to Dust

The gate for Missoula was at the end of the D concourse of the Salt Lake City airport, where flights to small western cities were departing every fifteen minutes. The gate area was thronged with large families, either greeting arrivals or mobilizing themselves for departure. Everyone seemed to be wearing shorts and carrying take-out food.

Celeste wondered if, in addition to Mac, who was flying in from the East, there would be others on the flight also attending the memorial. She was interested to see who Janet Pogue had invited and looked around the gate area for people she recognized. So far Celeste hadn't seen anyone who looked familiar. Hopefully, she and Mac would manage to retain the adjacent seats they had reserved in advance. The last time Celeste had made the same flight, it was oversold, in one of those brilliant airline strategies to serve the area without having any empty seats.

Celeste settled down with the thriller she was currently reading, but just as she managed to concentrate sufficiently to read a full page, she felt Mac's touch at the back of her neck. She turned around and stood up into his embrace. He kissed her lips with an enthusiastic smack and pulled her into a hug. His greeting was more affectionate than sexy, which pleasantly surprised Celeste.

"I'll greet you properly later," said Mac into her ear. He was obviously sensitive to making a scene.

Celeste grinned at Mac. She felt like a teenager in love with a grown-up. She was anticipating the pleasure of sitting next to Mac on the plane and feeling him brush against her. It was strange, thought Celeste, how planes crowded strangers into intimate contact, when a mere wink from a coworker could be classified as sexual harassment.

While they waited to board, Celeste and Mac caught up on their news. Without thinking that Mac might take it personally, Celeste told him the story of the condominium sale.

He looked like he wanted to say something when she told him she planned to make a bid on the place. But he seemed to be holding back and appeared uncomfortable.

To change the subject, Celeste managed to step into another landmine. She asked Mac if Russo had said anything about a job offer from BAU. Mac answered that Russo hadn't said anything specific, but he had implied that he might be looking at other positions where he could bring some junior people along with him.

"That would solve a big problem for us," he said.

"Well, the difficult side to it is that Grantham, my new chair, may have promised him *my* position to fill."

"She can't do that," said Mac.

"I wouldn't be so sure. She seems very determined to make it difficult for me to get promoted."

Then Celeste told Mac of the strange article that Harry had written her about, proposing the bioblaster theory. She even told him her private joke about the criminal being in cahoots with Grantham.

"If you're right or the French police are right, then the perfect target would be this flight. Not only will the rest of your referees be on it, but you will as well. That should definitely solve Grantham's problems," Mac pointed out in response.

They spent the remainder of the waiting period playing a game that Celeste sometimes played by herself when traveling to a scientific conference. She called it "spot the scientist." Traveling scientists usually stood out from the general crowd. They had a characteristic air of impatience. The easy ones to identify were reading manuscripts in some form or another—either already published in a journal, a photocopy thereof, or a printout they were editing to be submitted for publication from their own laboratory. The ones with a vindictive look were likely reviewing manuscripts from other people's laboratories that were being evaluated for publication. Given the predatory air of some reviewers Celeste had spotted, she was impressed that the system of peer review actually functioned and that manuscripts eventually did get published.

Disappointed, Celeste and Mac were not able to identify any candidates for attending Pogue's memorial service by the time the boarding announcement was made. However, about twenty minutes before they were due to land in Missoula, Celeste remembered Mac's comment about the flight being an ideal target for the bioblaster. The plane dropped precipitously, in an air pocket over the mountainous approach to the Bitterroot Valley. The entire plane-load of passengers whooped in reaction. Celeste would have been more concerned if the whoop hadn't recalled the previous time she had flown into Mis-soula. She realized that this turbulence was an ex-pected perk for most of the travelers. To the hardy residents of the Bitterroot Valley, the flight was the equivalent of an amusement park ride.

The plane from Salt Lake City to Missoula was not well designed for hand luggage. While Celeste and Mac waited at the baggage carousel for the appear-ance of the small bags they had checked, Celeste was prompted to remember another idiosyncrasy from her previous trip to the region. At the Missoula airport, the U.S. mail had precedence over the passengers' luggage. So when the mailbags started coming through on the carousel, Celeste realized that they would have another few minutes to wait for the bag-gage. She described her bag to Mac and then went over to the rental car counter to sort out their reser-vation. She was surprised to see Kirsten and Lars Lar-sen in the queue ahead of her.

They had just landed from Minneapolis. Even the Missoula airport operated under hub rules.

Kirsten kissed Celeste on the cheek and, peering over her shoulder, said, "I see you've brought that nice young man with you."

"I decided I liked him better than the French one," said Celeste.

Meanwhile, Larsen was raising a stink at the rental car counter. He had become positively pink with rage. "I don't care if you don't have our reservation. The fact is, I made one, so you better come up with a car PDQ."

"I'm sorry, sir, but everything we have is either out or reserved." The spotty complexion of the guy behind the counter indicated he couldn't have been older than twenty; probably younger than Larsen's son and a good deal more responsible, from what Celeste had heard. It was remarkable how the children of successful scientists were frequently ne'er-do-wells and, at best, underachievers.

Celeste butted in. "If you've got my reservation, we could all go together."

Larsen glared at her. Evidently he thought he was going to be able to make a car materialize by sheer persistence. Celeste was inhibiting that process.

"What's the name, ma'am?"

"Braun. Celeste Braun," answered Celeste, amused that in Montana she was ma'am, while in France she had been mademoiselle. Was her new attachment to Mac that obvious?

"Yeah, we got it."

"So you've got the last car in this godforsaken place," said Larsen to Celeste.

"I don't think it's the last car, but it sounds like the others are spoken for. Why don't you and Kirsten come with us?"

"Yes, Lars," commanded Kirsten. "That sounds like a good idea. I'm sure that if we need a car, you can rent one where we're staying. And it's only for two nights anyway."

Celeste noticed that Kirsten sounded uncharacter-istically authoritative. It was a behavior that didn't fit quite with either the flirtatious Kirsten or the self-indulgent Kirsten, both of whom Celeste had taken for granted.

Celeste's drive with Mac through the Bitterroot Valley was not exactly as she had daydreamed about it. For a start, Mac sat in the back with Kirsten Lar-sen, while Lars sulked silently in the passenger seat next to Celeste. However, even the extra company could not dampen Celeste's sense of exhilaration as the valley opened up before her, along the highway. Until Celeste's previous trip to the Bitterroot she had never believed that a person could immediately res-onate to a place. At that time, she had been a passen-ger, with her friend Debbie driving, and had felt an instant affinity for the wide horizons of Montana. A short time later, Celeste read Steinbeck's *Travels with Charley*, his story of driving cross-country with his poodle. She completely understood the opening sen-tence to his description of this segment of his trip: "I am in love with the state of Montana." Celeste had a recurrent sense that she would continue to return to Montana, and that this trip was part of a pattern.

Celeste and Debbie had stayed at the Millstone Wildlife Refuge on their previous trip. Debbie knew the area well, since she had been raised in the Bitter-root. She had booked the bed and breakfast at the refuge for a long weekend with a short-lived boy-friend. When the boyfriend canceled at the last min-ute, Debbie had invited Celeste, who was getting over Mac's departure at the time. However, not much had changed in the Bitterroot in the almost two years since then and Celeste easily remembered the landmarks at the turnoff to the refuge from the main road.

The refuge was a favorite place for guests of the nearby laboratory to stay and the perfect place for Janet Pogue's farewell to her husband. It had been established by a group of local wildlife enthusiasts, by persistent purchasing of contiguous farms bordering on the Bitterroot River, financed through a state-sanctioned conservation easement program. The largest farmhouse was run as a bed and breakfast and the smaller farmhouses were rented as vacation cottages.

Celeste stopped the car at the back of the large farmhouse, where the drive looped around a huge kitchen garden. As they pulled up, they were greeted by a short, sun-baked woman about Celeste's age, who was working in the garden. Celeste remembered the gardener from her previous visit, a spunky woman who had fled Detroit in her early twenties and spent her first years out west as a pool hustler in Wyoming.

The gardener, standing in for the manager, checked them in, which simply involved telling them where their rooms were and when to assemble for dinner. There were not many out-of-town guests attending the Pogue memorial, she told them. They were all accommodated in the bed and breakfast building, known as the Lodge, excepting Celeste and Mac who were assigned to the smallest farmhouse, about two hundred yards down the lane. Drinks would be served at seven thirty at the Lodge and they would all have dinner there. This gave them about an hour to settle in and wash up.

•   •   •

Celeste and Mac appreciated Janet Pogue's arrangements as they wandered up the lane back toward the Lodge from their private cottage. They'd indulged in what Mac playfully called a "nooner," as soon as they spotted the inviting brass bed in the upstairs bedroom at the cottage. Mac explained it was what his great-grandpa did when he lifted his great-grandma's skirts, after coming home from the office for lunch. He had told Mac's dad that it was a custom that had refreshed them both for the afternoon ahead. Mac and Celeste were also refreshed by their afternoon lovemaking, though the heat of the Montana day had yet to dissipate. The Bitterroot Range, bordering the valley, stretched across the horizon ahead of them. The mountains, still bearing patches of last winter's snow, were turning purple in the approaching dusk and promised a cool evening.

"I can see why the Pogues wanted to return to Montana," said Celeste.

Mac's response was to take her hand.

Thinking about the reason for their visit rekindled an anxiety that Celeste hadn't yet mentioned to Mac. "I hope that Ivan Rank isn't here. His pettiness would surely destroy this atmosphere."

"I doubt he would be," Mac reassured her. "There was no love lost between Rank and Pogue. I think Pogue was just being friendly to Wally Dyer at the meeting to stir the pot."

"Why would he stir the pot?"

"Well, your lab did scoop his with Meg's data last year. Maybe it pissed him off."

"I suppose you're right. But Janet said that the reason she invited me was because of Richard's respect for me."

"The two attitudes aren't mutually exclusive," said Mac.

"Anyway, Richard Pogue is dead, so his motivations are irrelevant."

"Nonetheless, even if Pogue liked him, I doubt Janet would have invited Rank. He's not particularly fond of women and I can guess that he completely ignored the importance of her contributions to Pogue's research. I'm pretty sure that Janet would invite only those who also had respect for her. Unfortunately, in our community, it's probably not a very large number."

Mac was right on all counts. When they arrived at the Lodge, Janet greeted them, saying, "Good, we're all here." Celeste looked around the room and, relieved, saw there was no sign of Rank. In fact, it was a very small gathering. In addition to the Larsens was Shelley Churchill, who looked positively blooming in spite of her recent widowhood. And next to Shelley Churchill, to Celeste's delight and surprise, stood her good friend Toshimi Matsumoto.

Toshimi, wearing suit trousers and a jacket, looked exactly as he would in Japan, except that he wasn't wearing a tie. His open collar was apparently a concession to the wild American West. He beamed, as he always did when he saw Celeste. He also had a remarkable second sense, and frequently answered Celeste's questions before she posed them.

"Richard Pogue loved our Japanese cuisine," he explained simply.

• • •

It was a congenial group whom Janet had summoned to pay their respects to her husband. Janet and Richard's two grown children and their grandchildren had remained behind at the Pogues' house, down the river a bit. Janet confessed that it was comforting to escape to the company of colleagues in this situation.

The refuge gardener had once again changed hats and acted as chef. Her daughter, pendulously pregnant, waited on tables. The dinner was delicious and, after dessert, the guests gravitated to one of the two sitting rooms to finish their wine or coffee, in comfortable conversation.

Toshimi took his fatherly responsibilities toward Celeste quite seriously and made a concerted effort to draw Mac into conversation. Once they discovered that Kazuko was a mutual friend, it was smooth sailing.

Larsen was completely out of his element, with no one to impress. He sat by himself, looking through the fishing records of guests at the Lodge and scowling.

In an almost Victorian reaction, Celeste decided that it would be best to let the men get on with their bonding or pouting, as the case may be. She poured herself another glass of wine and wandered to the other sitting room to which Janet, Shelley, and Kirsten had purposefully retreated.

". . . might look like murder," Celeste heard Shelley saying as she walked into the room. The three women looked up, almost furtively. They seemed to be worried that they were talking about something that shouldn't be discussed.

"Oh, dear," said Celeste. "I hope the police haven't been bothering you."

"What makes you say that?" asked Janet. She sounded stressed.

"A reporter friend of mine sent me a bizarre article, presumably from the French gutter press. I told him it was a pile of crap."

"That's exactly what we were talking about," said Janet. "As if Shelley and I didn't have enough to concern us."

"At least Shelley already has a separate identity," said Kirsten.

Celeste was puzzled by this remark and wondered if it was a reference to Shelley's tendency to dress with flamboyant emphasis on her excellent figure. It was a tendency that Celeste had always attributed to Shelley's competition with her late husband George's constant bid for attention. Since Celeste had last seen Shelley at the memorial service for George, Shelley had her hair cut into a short feathered cap that suited her diminutive, well-endowed body and made her more attractive than ever.

"Kirsten, you make my 'separate identity' sound much more meaningful than it is in reality," protested Shelley. "You know I reverted to my maiden name when the kids left home; because I started to help out my father with his travel agency. It was like going from the frying pan into the fire, from being Mrs. George Churchill to being a dutiful daughter again. Now they're both gone, so at least I can be me once more."

"Come on, you two," admonished Janet. "We can't

have dissent in the shadow cabinet. I came here this evening to get away from squabbling."

"Sorry, Janet," said Kirsten. "I just meant you might have a harder time establishing yourself. Only by name, of course."

"I've never been out to establish myself, Kirsten. Only to fulfill myself. But, in either case, the diversion is now gone. I had no idea when I got involved with Richard when we were both freshmen at the university in Missoula that I'd be postponing my goals for this long."

The raw candor of these women dismayed Celeste. Clearly falling in love later in life was preferable to having settled down with a college sweetheart. She felt incredibly fortunate.

Many of the scientists at the lab where Richard Pogue had been director lived in the Bitterroot Valley for the fly-fishing. Consequently, Janet was easily able to find owners of inflatable fishing rafts who were willing to help out with the trip down the Bitterroot. Janet, with her son and daughter, was piloted by her teenage grandson in their family raft, at the rear of the flotilla, quietly leaving a trail of ashes behind them. Three staff members from the labs piloted the other rafts. At the front were Celeste, Toshimi, and Mac. They were followed by Shelley, Kirsten, and Lars, who preceded a raft carrying Janet's two younger grandchildren with their other parents.

The Bitterroot's flow was deceptively gentle and the rafts glided easily between the islands of river rubble and twisted tree trunks whose existence attested to a rougher time of year. In deference to the occasion, the raft occupants were quiet, surrendering to the river's flux. Being in the first raft, Celeste had the added treat of seeing the local birds before they were disturbed by the others. The birds of the Bitterroot were ones with character—cedar waxwings, kingfishers, pink and green Lewis's woodpeckers, and the fishermen's competition, ospreys. Their flitting and soaring was a fitting accompaniment to the procession. Celeste observed them contentedly with her field glasses. At one point, Celeste looked back at the procession behind them and caught the expression on Janet Pogue's face. The river had charmed even the grieving widow into an expression of serene contentment.

Toshimi said, "I have only seen one river in Japan which can equal this. It is the Shimanto-gawa, crossed by the Yodo train line, in the mountains of Shikoku. Like this river, it is more strong than the land. Perhaps you will have a chance to see this, Celeste, when you come to Shikoku next month. Our conference is at Ashizuri-Misaki, the cape at the southwest tip of Shikoku. The Yodo line leaves from Kubokawa Station, in the mountains north of Ashizuri. But Ashizuri is also very beautiful. You must take time to see it. And, of course, we want you to come see us at the new division in Tokushima, after the meeting."

"All this sounds wonderful, Toshimi," replied Celeste. "But I have been traveling so much. If I took time to see everything interesting, I would never be home. It is a critical time for me to be concerned about writing manuscripts."

"Is this because of your situation at work or because you might be feeling some competition?"

"Both, actually," answered Celeste, glad she did not have to be too explicit. Toshimi was on the list of suggested referees she'd given to Grantham.

"I think I know about the competition," said Toshimi. "I had an unusual fax from Dr. Ivan Rank last week. He said he did not want you to speak in his session, but if I insisted, then he would speak before you. I am afraid I insisted."

"Thank you, Toshimi. And thank you for telling me about it." Celeste sighed.

"The best thing about the conference hotel at Ashizuri," said Toshimi, in an effort to change the subject, "is the bath. The one that is very hot is outside, looking over the cliffs of the cape. This time we must take a bath together." The remark referred to a long-standing personal joke between them. Early in their acquaintanceship they had tried to bathe at Noboribetsu Hot Springs on the island of Hokkaido, but the men and women's baths were not segregated and no one in their polite group dared follow through. "Unfortunately, the men and women each have their own cliff at Ashizuri," Toshimi reassured her, perhaps for Mac's sake.

He then turned to Mac, who was lazily enjoying the sensation of floating along in Celeste's company. "Mac, you should come to Ashizuri, also. The work you are doing with Dr. Russo that you told me of last night would be very much of interest. Dr. Russo is coming, too, but he has many things he can talk about. With George and Richard gone, we have big holes in our program. Janet will, of course, speak in Richard's place, but you would also be very welcome."

"That is kind of you, Toshimi," said Mac. "I would enjoy seeing that part of Japan very much."

"Then it is settled. I will send you a fax about the registration and program when I return. Do I need to worry about the accommodation?"

Mac and Celeste looked at each other. Toshimi seemed to be giving his blessing. "I don't think so," responded Celeste, turning slightly pink.

"Very good," Toshimi said and smiled.

Later, after the farewell float trip terminated with an early evening barbecue, Celeste and Mac sat out on the verandah of the cottage where they were staying. Small bats were darting in and out of the light leaking from the interior of the cottage, keeping the area insect free.

"After Toshimi's invitation today, I feel as though I have your family's approval," said Mac.

"For what?"

"For wanting to marry you."

"Is that what you want?"

"Don't you?"

"I don't know, Mac. It has crossed my mind."

"Then let's do it. I'm crazy about you and get pretty good vibes from you in return."

"You know I'm crazy about you, too," said Celeste. "It's just that . . ."

"What? You've never thought of yourself as the marrying kind?" Mac's tone was slightly disdainful.

"Well, you don't have to mock me," answered Celeste defensively. "You have to admit that the marriages with or between scientists that we've known are hardly exemplary."

"It would be different for us," said Mac. "Times have changed and we're both independent from the start. Or if anything, I'm more dependent on you."

"I suppose you being male automatically means you'd have an easier time than someone like Janet."

"Anyway, aren't you concerned that you'll soon be past child-bearing age?"

"I don't feel the need to breed," said Celeste. She'd long ago been convinced that this was one biological urge that was easily overcome.

"I don't see it as a need," said Mac. "I loved raising Mac Junior and now he's almost ready to go to college. It would be wonderful to have you as the mother of my second child. And even more so, to share it with you. That's one of my few regrets about splitting up with Martha."

"Oh, Mac. I don't know what to say. You're asking me to go from being a single woman to den mother, all in one go. Shouldn't we at least see if we can get jobs in the same city?"

"If you say you'll marry me and that you'll at least think about having my child."

"Is that blackmail?"

"Just persuasion," said Mac, rising from his wicker chair. He walked over to Celeste, stood behind her, and started to massage her neck. He could feel two knots of tension between her shoulder blades. He realized she must be more worried about committing herself than he'd thought. He said, "If we were married, I could do this every night. And this." He bent down and kissed her neck. "And this." He moved his hands slowly down her chest.

Celeste could feel her nipples tighten in response,

and she thought of the surgical slash across Janet Pogue's breast. Life is short and unpredictable. Why was she feeling so reluctant?

"I guess you're right—I won't have to worry about being in the shadow cabinet," she said, relaxing under the influence of Mac's caress.

"Huh?"

"It's what Shelley, Kirsten, and Janet call themselves."

"Well, they don't have such a bad time." Mac had maneuvered himself around to Celeste's front and, pulling her up into his arms, began gently to kiss her face.

Celeste drew back, savoring the moment before being drawn inevitably into lovemaking. "How do you mean?"

"Well, I saw Shelley Churchill's behavior at the ski resort. During the conference she seemed to be a regular visitor at the staff lodge. Obviously that was before her husband died." He paused to kiss Celeste again. "I wouldn't be surprised if she was up to something like I'm about to do with you." Mac held out his hand to lead Celeste up to the bedroom.

A good while later, while they were lying in bed, having completely sated each other, Celeste and Mac were engaged to be married.

8

Wet Wrecks

Celeste walked out onto the cliff stark naked and stood on a wet stone step high above the Pacific Ocean, at the southernmost point of Shikoku. It was only three weeks since she and Mac were betrothed and Celeste was still getting used to the idea. The sharp breeze felt good on her skin, which was flushed from the hottest bath indoors. She recalled Toshimi's warning that the bath outdoors was even hotter, as she stepped down one shallow step into the stone pool before her. In a few seconds she would have to immerse herself to stay warm, but for a suspended moment Celeste savored the contrast between her throbbing feet and cooling body, looking down at the violet waves of the ocean below. The design of the site was brilliant. It was completely private so that a bather could stand without being seen, but could see for miles out over the sea. From Celeste's vantage point, the Ashizuri-Misaki lighthouse was just visible on the bit of coast jutting out below the cliffs, which were sparsely decorated with scrubby shrubs. To Celeste's right was a wooden fence masking another cliff-top pool, accessible from the men's side of the hotel baths. There would be no view of the lighthouse from that side. With typical Japanese courtesy, the different sides of the baths were alternately assigned to men and women on different days, so that any guest staying more than one night would be able to have the lighthouse view from the baths at least once.

Celeste was alone in this exposed but secret place and relished the solitude. She needed to think and hadn't had the opportunity since Mac had joined her in San Francisco for the trans-Pacific trip. They had been met by Toshimi at the Osaka airport after their ten-hour flight. The three of them then caught a bus to the ferry across the Inland Sea and, from the ferry, they endured a long train ride, followed by a jolting bus ride, to the hotel site. Celeste fell asleep on the ferry and slept most of the rest of the journey. Her fatigue had spared her from succumbing to the sea-sickness afflicting most of the passengers on the rough Inland Sea crossing. Toshimi and Mac were not so lucky and had the added difficulty of trying to remain polite while they disguised their discomfort. Waking up between naps throughout their trip, Celeste could see that both were looking rather green and strained. Their appearance did not improve for the duration.

Upon arrival, Toshimi used conference arrangements as an excuse to retire. Mac was equally determined to lie down. As soon as the chambermaid closed the sliding door to the *tatami*-covered room assigned to Mac and Celeste, Mac made straight for the cupboard where the futons were stored. Protocol and manners were not a high priority as he flopped a

futon on the floor and stretched himself out with a
groan. Celeste escaped to the baths for refreshment,
hoping to stay awake through the evening dinner.

The first problem Celeste needed to sort through
was the upcoming encounter with Ivan Rank. As she
slowly eased herself into the cliff-top bath, she re-
flected that speaking at tomorrow morning's session
at the conference would have a lot in common with
steeling herself against the sting of the hot water.
Rank would be chairing the session and, as Toshimi
had forewarned, had been adamant about taking the
chair's prerogative to give the first talk. Celeste was
seriously concerned that his data would preempt her
contribution, which would follow. She had seen this
happen often enough to others and had observed that
the second speaker could usually save face by being
gracious about the previous speaker's similar work.
She was determined to adhere to this formulaic courtesy but it would take some ad hoc inventiveness on
her part. She had to accept that there was no way to
prepare adequately for her own talk, since she wasn't
sure what Rank would say. The uncertainty was disquieting.

The second issue on Celeste's mind was Mac.
Well, it wasn't exactly Mac who worried her. It was
Harry Freeman, who had taken her by surprise. When
Celeste had returned from Montana, she had phoned
Harry to tell him about her engagement to Mac. He
had sounded genuinely pleased for her and went on
to chat about other subjects. Celeste recalled their joc-
ular discussion about the bioblaster theory of the
French police, and, on the surface, it had seemed like
things were unchanged between them. Then, the day

before she left for Japan, Celeste received a long and heartrending handwritten letter from Harry about not wanting to lose her as a friend, stating that she was the only person in his cynical life he had ever had strong feelings for. Reading between the lines, Harry sounded as devastated as a jilted fiancé. Celeste was distressed that she had caused him distress and began to question her haste in committing to Mac. Her doubts, of course, had been completely dispelled as soon as Mac's arms were around her when he arrived later that afternoon. But Harry's evident pain was nonetheless disturbing.

Celeste took a deep breath of the chilly evening air and massaged her feet under the water. It was strange how if she sat perfectly still, she could tolerate the heat, but as soon as she moved a limb, it felt scalding. When she could stand it no longer, Celeste lifted herself halfway out of the pool to sit on the cold stone edge. Her thoughts had just returned to marriage, when the door from the baths opened and Kazuko stepped out into the cool dusk. Her slender body was steaming and she looked like a vision.

"I thought I might find you here," said Kazuko. "It is very inspirational."

Celeste observed that Kazuko went through the same ritual as she had, first gazing out to sea and enjoying the breeze, then sliding with mixed relief and shock into the pool.

"It's a good place for thinking," said Celeste.

"You must be very happy," said Kazuko warmly. "Toshimi told me about you and Mac. I am very pleased. He is a good man."

"Thank you. I'm glad you think so."

"I wanted to say something between us, before the widows are here. We will not be alone, shortly," said Kazuko, "They are in the inside baths and will come out. Toshimi was very kind to invite Shelley Churchill to be with Janet Pogue, who will speak in her husband's place. Kirsten Larsen is with them also."

"Yes, they are remarkably close. I suppose it's a bond of similar experience."

"You will not have that experience of marriage. You and Mac will be like me with Akira."

Kazuko and Akira had shared a lab at Fukuda Pharmaceuticals. His murder, two years earlier, had brought Kazuko and Celeste together. This was the first time since his death that Kazuko had mentioned her late husband by name to Celeste. Celeste responded, with a tangible lump in her throat, "It would be a great privilege if we are."

"I think these ladies are more close to each other than to their husbands," observed Kazuko. "So, in some way, they still experience a special relationship. When I came into the bath they were sitting together in the deep wood tub, whispering like naughty children. Like they were planning trouble. They even looked guilty when I went to welcome them. I asked, 'What is the secret?' and they laughed."

"Here they come now." The door from the bath opened and Kirsten came out, followed by Janet and Shelley.

"Here's Kazuko," said Kirsten. "Maybe she'll know."

"And here's Celeste," said Janet and a round of greeting began.

When this was over and all three had entered the

pool with various expressions about the heat, Kazuko asked, "What did you think I would know?"

"We would really like to go on the dive trip, but weren't sure we would be allowed, since we just want to snorkel," explained Shelley.

"I am sure there will be no problem," said Kazuko. "We have chartered a commercial fishing boat from the harbor and there is space for everyone at the meeting. But I do not think everyone will want to go."

"Well, that's a relief," said Kirsten. "Lars is such an authoritative ass, when it comes to diving. He told me that the deep dive captains never allow amateurs on their boats, since they get in the way of the 'serious' divers."

"On the contrary," said Kazuko. "None of the commercial captains wanted to take the deep-divers. Toshimi had to find an expert to come along to be responsible."

"Yes, I was wondering about that," said Kirsten. "The deep dives that Lars usually does are special, exclusive charters. They're all macho men and apparently behave like animals when they're not swimming around the wrecks. When they're at the wrecks, they treat the dive like a navy mission."

"It's a rather bizarre form of entertainment—to get your kicks from swimming around past disasters," remarked Shelley.

"I think the kick comes from the danger of the depth, as much as from seeing the wrecks. Of course, there's the added potential danger of finding an ammunition room or of getting trapped in the wreckage by a bloodthirsty shark," Kirsten replied.

Shelley looked thoughtful and then said, with evident rancor, "I guess it's not that different from the supposed thrill of skiing down an unmarked slope."

The women in the pool were silent. It was a strangely exclusive silence that caused Celeste and Kazuko to look at each other with conspiratorial glances. They rose simultaneously from the pool to retreat to the coziness of the indoor baths.

The hotel had a small well-appointed lecture hall on the basement level, where the conference was held. Rank's session was the first one and Celeste decided to show up a few minutes early with the hope of talking to Rank before they began. The room was empty when Celeste arrived and she sat down in the front row to load her slides into the holder, labeled with her name, that had been laid out on a table next to the projector. The conference room gradually filled up and many of the participants greeted Celeste as they found their seats. There was still no sign of Rank until Toshimi began his welcoming speech. Then Rank rushed in and sat down in the front row, on the opposite side of the hall from Celeste. He did not look around to locate the speakers in his session, but stared straight ahead. His expression was pained and his movements bordered on the manic. Celeste's discomfort increased. She began to worry that he might make a negative personal remark about her. He had a reputation for flying off the handle and verbally attacking coworkers in his laboratory when he became frustrated with them. This had occurred more than once during the period that Celeste had worked in his lab as an undergraduate, though she had never witnessed one of these tantrums firsthand.

However, Rank was enough of a showman that the desire to impress his audience was greater than his desire to discredit Celeste. The imperious manner in which he delivered his talk revealed his confidence that his data would speak for itself. It was obvious that he intended to establish his dominance in the emerging research field that his laboratory had just joined.

Celeste listened with rapt attention. The suspense was agonizing. She had to wait patiently while Rank gave a long introduction describing the evidence that many types of virus had different mechanisms for evading an immune response against them. He painstakingly defined his early role in demonstrating that virus mutation was a major contributor to their ability to escape recognition by white blood cells and antibodies that develop to fight an infection. He finally moved on to the topic that had brought him and Celeste into competition. This he also presented in pedantic detail.

He cited the evidence that particular strains of virus had evolved genes that encoded proteins that could specifically sabotage the establishment of an immune response. These proteins actively prevented the stimulation of immunity. Celeste almost held her breath when he began to talk about the ability of virus proteins to make MHC molecules disappear. His laboratory was measuring disappearance using a different criterion than Karen had used in Celeste's laboratory, but fundamentally they were looking at the same phenomenon. The MHC molecules were needed to display fragments of viral protein so that they were recognizable by T cells. Without these molecules, the virus essentially became invisible to the immune system.

Rank mentioned Wally Dyer's critical contribution to the experiment, which allowed them to clone the virus gene responsible for MHC disappearance. Then he showed a slide with the gene sequence and a diagram of its predicted protein product. Dyer's gene was completely different from the gene that Karen had cloned.

As she absorbed the data on the slide, Celeste instantly understood what was going on. She immediately relaxed and smiled involuntarily with relief as Rank began to conclude his lecture. Though he had not looked at her throughout his talk, he looked at her triumphantly as he clicked to the slide of his summary remarks and caught her fading smile. This sight caused him to blanch and break his momentum. He awkwardly stumbled through the list of points on his slide, losing the impact of what he had intended as a dramatic finale.

There were several questions at the conclusion of Rank's talk and he answered them with lengthy speculative responses, encouraging further questions, which cut considerably into the time scheduled for Celeste's talk. When he could induce no more probing from the audience, he reluctantly and briefly introduced Celeste as "Dr. Celeste Braun, Assistant Professor at Bay Area University, who will speak on the same topic." He laid definitive stress on the title of *assistant*.

Celeste was not the least bit disturbed. She began cheerfully. "I am grateful to Ivan for the thorough background he has presented, since it is relevant to both our talks. Consequently, I will be able to skip over several of my early slides and maybe even get us back on track for a coffee break. I am also grateful to Ivan for the training I had in his laboratory when I was an undergraduate. No doubt his influence played a role in the thinking that led me to pursue the investigation I will discuss today." Rank's face turned an unnatural color.

"As Ivan mentioned, viruses that establish chronic infections are ones that have mechanisms for evading an immune response. One of the most insidious of these is cytomegalovirus, or CMV. Many of us harbor CMV and a healthy immune system can live with it, keeping it under control. But when a patient's immune system is weakened, as in HIV infection or following treatment for cancer or organ transplantation, CMV infection can expand out of control. Karen Klein in my laboratory has discovered the reason for CMV's exceptionally successful immune evasion. She has found genetic evidence for at least six distinct gene products that interfere with the expression and function of MHC molecules. I will now show you the data on the location of these genes within the virus genome and will present the details about one of them that we have cloned. You have just heard from Ivan about one of the others whose location we have mapped. It's a relief to hear that we now have only four more to characterize."

The expression on Ivan Rank's face indicated that he was neither amused nor gratified that his data and Celeste's were complementary. He and Dyer had completely missed the fact that there were a number of different immune evasion genes.

Celeste finished her talk just slightly over the originally scheduled time limit, making up for most of the time that Rank had exceeded his. But Rank jumped up and said abruptly, "We don't have time for questions, if we want to keep on schedule."

There were several hands raised in the audience. Toshimi leaned forward from the front row and said, in an uncharacteristically loud voice, "The coffee will wait. I think you can allow one question."

Rank looked impatient and remained standing, while Celeste acknowledged one of the raised hands.

"This is a fascinating finding, but why do you think there is redundancy in the virus genes for this immune evasion behavior?" The query came from Nick Russo, Mac's boss.

It was a perfect question, highlighting the importance of Celeste's lab's contribution. She explained her hypothesis that it was a strategy on the part of the virus to deal with variation in the human population among MHC molecules. If the virus could target several different steps in MHC function, then it would be more effective against human variants. She was about to discuss the issue of coevolution of humans and pathogens when Rank interrupted.

"I think you should pursue this discussion during the break. We don't want to cut into any more of the time for the next talk," said Rank. He continued with an introduction to the next speaker before Celeste even had time to step down from the podium. Rank's behavior was so rude and so obvious that Celeste was embarrassed for him.

As she only half-listened to the next speaker, Celeste rehearsed how she might approach Rank to discuss submission of their work for publication. Often, in such situations when two laboratories made complementary discoveries, it was customary to submit papers to be considered for "back-to-back" publication in the same journal. But this involved cooperation between the laboratories involved. It would be critical to find out where Rank and Dyer's manuscript stood, since Karen was just finalizing the data for the submission from Celeste's lab.

However, as soon as the session was over, Rank bolted from the conference hall. Celeste tried to follow him out, but he had disappeared by the time she reached the room exit. She learned later, from Toshimi at lunch, that during the coffee break, Rank had made a huge fuss at the hotel reception desk. He demanded that they help him change his return reservation to the next possible flight he could make from Osaka back to New York.

Celeste understood that this meant a race to publication. All she could hope for was that the papers might appear within a few weeks of each other. It wasn't uncommon that related publications, even if they were in different journals, were discussed jointly in the news section of one of the top journals. When the manuscript from her laboratory was submitted for publication, she could alert the journal to the possible appearance of Rank and Dyer's paper. This might at least encourage a rapid review and possibly a news commentary, if her manuscript was accepted. She faxed a message to Karen about what she had heard from Rank and instructed her to start drafting the manuscript as soon as the data figures were completed.

• • •

Although the situation with respect to Rank's work had turned out far better than Celeste had imagined it would, the tension of the continued competition affected her ability to relax and enjoy the rest of the conference. She was grateful that there had been only two days of scheduled talks. It had been difficult to concentrate on other people's science when she was so anxious to get her own sorted out. Celeste hoped that the dive trip on the following day would dispel her impatience to get home. She was trying not to regret her promise to visit the new branch of Fukuda in Tokushima before she and Mac headed home to opposite sides of the country. Toshimi was so evidently proud of this new facility and so anxious to show his acceptance of Mac that an early return home was absolutely out of the question.

Celeste was thinking these thoughts while sitting in the hotel bar, where Lars Larsen was loudly describing his diving exploits to Mac. Celeste, Mac, and Kazuko had been enjoying a quiet drink when Larsen, accompanied by the three wives, joined them. In desperate need of a male ear, he cornered Mac. One of Larsen's dive buddies was a Vietnam veteran who had stayed on in the Far East and specialized in leading trips to explore wrecks from the Second World War. Larsen seemed to think that Mac might have run across him during his own service in Vietnam. Not surprisingly, Mac did not know the man. Celeste wondered how Mac felt being reminded of his war experiences as though they were jolly college days that he had shared with friends. She was impressed by his tolerance of Larsen's harangue.

"The trip tomorrow will make my dive buddies really jealous," boasted Larsen. "Last time we went after the Japanese wrecks in Truk Lagoon, they were talking about this site off Shikoku. They'll hardly believe I got the chance to check it out because of my work." He paused to take a sip of soda water. Larsen had already explained the prohibition of alcohol the night before a deep dive.

"What's so great about this site?" asked Mac, with resignation. He might at least discover the clue to Larsen's obsession.

"Well, for one thing, it's two hundred feet to the decks—at least as deep as the Truk Lagoon dives. For another thing, in addition to the Japanese craft down there, there's supposedly a U.S. sub down there that got caught in one of our own mines."

Mac raised his eyebrows in what was meant to be a knowing acknowledgment. He was fully familiar with the tendency of the U.S. military to self-destruct. But Larsen interpreted Mac's expression as one of surprise and it never took much prompting for Larsen to share his detailed knowledge of the Pacific war arena.

He took an anticipatory breath and then began. "You see, by early 1945, when the small bombing raids on the Japanese coastal cities were well under way, we had forced much of the Japanese shipping through the Inland Sea. Then we laid some strategic mines on their common supply routes. Apparently, one of our reconnaissance subs got diverted into one of them, but it was hushed up at the time. Those military records finally became public domain, on the fiftieth anniversary of the end of the war. After that, it took many dives to even locate the wreck. So it's practically unexplored. A pristine wreck is a deep diver's dream."

Mac was trying to come to grips with the concept of a pristine wreck, when Celeste rose from the table.

"I'm ready to turn in," she announced. "The dive trip starts even earlier than the conference sessions."

"Even the lowly snorkeler needs to sleep," agreed Mac, glad to be rescued from the next chapter of the Larsen version of U.S. military history.

"That's us," said Shelley Churchill, also rising and disbanding the rest of Larsen's audience. "We are the lowly snorkelers."

Celeste and Mac walked down the long green-carpeted corridor to their bedroom. They removed their shoes in the small entryway and slid open the door to the inner room. During dinner, their futons had been made up by the chambermaids, and there was a clean *yukata* laid out on each one. Celeste was not accustomed to the chronic presence of someone else in her room during a conference and she found it took some accommodation.

"You can use the bathroom first," she commanded.

"Okay," said Mac, catching her tone.

Celeste opened the window at the far end of the room and stood gazing out over the sea, which was well lit by a gibbous moon. She listened to Mac brushing his teeth, registering that it was a sound that would become comfortably familiar in no time at all.

Mac found her still by the window when he emerged from the bathroom wearing his *yukata*. He came up behind her and hugged her around the waist, nuzzling the back of her neck. "What's on your mind?" he asked.

"I don't know. I'm just tense from everything being so unresolved."

"What's everything? You have me."

"Mmm. But Rank is really worrying me and then there's the tenure situation and then, on top of that, there's the house in San Francisco. I'm going to have to make my bid within a week of getting back."

Mac let go of her abruptly, with surprise. "That's the first you've mentioned it to me."

"No, it isn't. I told you about it on the way to Montana. They're going through two rounds of bidding and the first one is when I return from Japan."

"I thought we were planning to live together," said Mac.

"We are. But one place we might live is in San Francisco. I'd be foolish not to make a bid. There will be a second round after their counteroffer anyway, so I can always drop out."

"You might have been less secretive about it," said Mac. "Don't I get some input into where we'll raise our children?"

"Oh, Mac," said Celeste with frustration. "Get real. You can't genuinely think that having children at this stage in our lives is a good idea. Besides, you've already had the satisfaction of doing it. Personally, I've never been that interested in giving up my freedom to be an adult. It took me so long to get to be my own person. Plus, you're forty-seven now. You'd turn sixty while any offspring were going through adolescence. Is that how you want to spend your life with me?"

"I never realized our age difference bothered you so much." He sounded hurt and angry.

"I'm sorry, Mac. I'm exhausted. This is something we should talk about under more relaxed circumstances. Let's get a good night's sleep and try to enjoy tomorrow. Hopefully we'll get some time to ourselves in the next couple of days." Privately, Celeste knew that being left alone was not compatible with the Japanese hospitality they were about to experience, but these were the only reassuring words she could think of. There was certainly no point in continuing the discussion at that moment.

"Whatever," said Mac sullenly and shrugged his shoulders. He went over to his futon and squatted down next to it, flipping the cover back. As Celeste picked up her *yukata* and headed for the bathroom, Mac switched off the light sitting on the floor adjacent to his futon, undid the sash of his *yukata,* and crawled under the futon cover. When Celeste came out of the bathroom, Mac's eyes were shut. She decided not to disturb him.

9

Gas and Geishas

The fishing boat chartered for the dive trip was pale yellow. It was one of a fleet of similar boats bobbing gently in the harbor. The boat fittings on deck, as well as the wooden lockers for the wet suits and snorkeling equipment, were also painted pale yellow and inscribed with black Japanese characters. In bright contrast, the divers' tanks, secured with bungee cords alongside one of the lockers, were painted in a rainbow of colors. Some of them were labeled around their necks with red or blue tags, which fluttered festively in the slight breeze. As the boat left the harbor, Celeste inhaled the fresh sea air and enjoyed Mac's warm presence beside her on the deck. It was impossible to stay angry with someone who had awakened her by making love. Celeste had such a strong sense of compatibility with Mac that she was confident they would be able to resolve their different goals. But that would happen as they became closer friends over time. Meanwhile there was plenty to appreciate in the romantic phase. Celeste sighed with rare contentment. Today was a day to forget about Ivan Rank and academic angst and enjoy being at sea with her lover.

About twenty of the conference participants and their assorted companions had stayed on for the diving excursion. They stood in groups and chatted, while the boat chugged cheerfully out to sea. There were four crew running the trip: the captain, the deep-dive master, the shallow-dive master, and the head of dive operations, who was also looking after the snorkelers. Celeste guessed that over half of the passengers would be scuba diving, judging by the number of gas cylinders on board. Scientists seemed to be attracted by technical sports.

The head of dive operations was gradually making the rounds, instructing each group of scientists how the dive trip would be organized. He was a grizzled sailor of indeterminant age, wearing an immaculate pale yellow jumpsuit. His face was so lined that his eyes almost disappeared. He spoke excellent English, possibly due to his association with his two dive masters, an Australian man and woman. The Australians looked to Celeste like atypically healthy transplants from the Haight-Ashbury neighborhood of San Francisco, but their accents were pure "Oz." The head of dive operations approached Kazuko, who was talking with Kirsten, Janet, and Shelley, near the row of dive tanks. They called Celeste and Mac over to join them for the briefing.

"Sata-san is the head of the dive operation," said Kazuko by way of introduction. "He will explain how the dives will be arranged."

Sata-san shook hands with all of them. "Welcome to the Inland Sea," he said. "We will arrive at the shelf in about forty-five minutes. We will drop anchor near a very shallow part where some can snorkel. There is also a ledge for the shallow dive. It is not far from the deep place with the submarine. You should have your wet suits on by the time we stop and assemble on the lower deck where the ladders are. On the lower deck, we will divide. Yvonne will explain to the shallow divers and Bill will instruct the deep divers. I will show the rest where to snorkel."

"I think we will all snorkel," said Kazuko, gesturing around the immediate group.

"Maybe," said Janet. "I'm not feeling great."

"How many will go on the deep dive?" asked Mac, with a slight twinge of envy.

"You can tell that," said Kirsten officiously. "All the tanks with red tags are the deep-dive helium-oxygen mix. Lars and the rest went to verify their mix yesterday at the dive shop. They write their name on the tank tag, once it has been checked. Oxygen gauges are one of the infinite pieces of equipment they accumulate."

"So the tanks with no tags are for the shallow divers?" asked Janet.

"That is almost correct," said Sata-san. "The no-tag tanks hold air, also for the first stage of the deep dive. The deep divers then switch tanks after one hundred feet to the second tank, with less oxygen than air. Also, some shallow divers have certification for nitrox, a nitrogen-oxygen mix with more oxygen than air. Those are blue-tag tanks. Of course, we have spares of all tanks in case of valve trouble." He pointed across the upper deck to the metal locker at the opposite end. "That locker over there has the wet suits and equipment for the snorkelers. You may try them to find a fit."

All but Janet started to move over to the far locker. "I need to visit the head," she said and rushed to the door leading to the area under the bridge, where the head was located.

"Poor Janet," said Kirsten. "The sea is quite different from rafting on a river."

"It could be the medication," replied Shelley in a whisper, which Celeste overheard as she moved toward the wet-suit locker. Though Celeste found it unnerving to look at Janet's disfigured breast, she had not wanted to appear to be averting her eyes when they were bathing a few days earlier, and she had noticed a new scar on Janet's intact breast. At the time she had wondered if routine biopsies were done to ensure that the cancer was still dormant. Celeste fervently hoped that Janet wasn't going through a new scare, on top of having to cope with Richard's death.

Celeste's worrying was diverted by the task of wriggling in and out of wet suits. It didn't take long before they were all reduced to helpless giggles, watching each other jump about trying to ease the recalcitrant second skins over their bathing suits. Celeste, Mac, and Kazuko were reasonably fitted. Kirsten and Shelley decided that they were altogether the wrong shape and resigned themselves to keeping Janet company. Later, just before the dive briefings began, Celeste returned to the upper deck to use the head. She saw that Kirsten, Shelley, and Janet had found three deck chairs and had settled themselves like passengers on a cruise ship. They looked so content that Celeste was reminded of Kazuko's obser-

vation about their special friendship, stimulated by
sharing the curse of insufferable husbands. Perhaps
their friendship was the secret of their endurance.

The reef in the Inland Sea didn't have the diversity
of marine life typical of reefs in warmer water, but
there was plenty to appreciate. Celeste always enjoyed the silence of being immersed in water and the
privileged view of a private world that a diving mask
afforded. It was easy to lose one's sense of definition
and merge with the underwater environment. After
close to an hour of exploring the upper surface of the
reef, Celeste followed Kazuko back to the ship's lad-
der and climbed onto the metal mesh platform that
served as the divers' access to the sea. The two of
them and Mac had been swimming together, occasionally gesturing to each other to point out various
underwater sights. Mac followed Celeste up the lad-
der and all three stood dripping and breathing hard.
    Celeste sensed immediately that something was
amiss. There were several divers on the platform, but
there was none of the whooping and shouting that had
accompanied the start of the dives. Sata-san was suit-
ing up with Yvonne's help. Celeste looked up to the
upper deck and saw Toshimi standing with Shelley,
Janet, and Kirsten. Janet had her arm around Kirsten's
shoulders. Sata-san said something to Kazuko sharply
in Japanese.
    "It's Larsen," said Kazuko to Celeste and Mac. "He
has not come up. Sata-san will go down to look for
him."
    "Didn't he have a buddy?" asked Celeste.
    "They split up to take photos, yeah?" said Yvonne.

"His buddy swam into one hole in the sub and Larsen swam into another. Larsen didn't come out the other end by the time the buddy had to come up. Now you three had better get up on deck and get dry. You're the last of the snorkelers and we'll need the platform clear."

Thirty minutes after Celeste, Mac, and Kazuko had changed and joined the crowd on the upper deck, Lars Larsen's body reached the surface of the Inland Sea. A respectful silence fell as the lifeless body bobbed into view with inappropriate caprice. The body was attached to a large, neon-orange balloon, which must have been filled with air by Sata-san, so it could rise and drag the body up with it. In spite of this clever device, it seemed contrary to the laws of physics that Larsen's heavily equipped body had been converted to a piece of flotsam.

Kazuko broke the silence. "Where is Sata-san?"

"He's still on the ascent line," answered one of the scientists who had done the deep dive. "The lift bag, that balloonlike thing, makes it possible for a body to be retrieved with all the equipment. Once it's inflated, it rises rapidly. But Sata-san has to come up more slowly and time his decompression stops as he moves up the ascent line."

"I can't figure what happened," said the deep diver who had been Larsen's buddy. "We all switched to the heliox tanks at one hundred feet. He gave me the thumbs up, so I know he was fine at that point."

"For God's sake," Kirsten said fiercely. "Can you shut up about it?"

"Come on, Kirsten," said Shelley. She and Janet ushered Kirsten off to the side, away from the bulk of the crowd. Celeste watched them put a blanket around Kirsten's shoulders. Janet then went to fetch a can of soft drink for her, from the cooler on deck.

"Why do you use a helium-oxygen mix?" Mac asked the diver when the wives were out of range.

"The helium is used to replace nitrogen, which is in air and other shallow-dive mixes, to avoid nitrogen narcosis. Also, for dives below one hundred feet, the percentage of oxygen has to be reduced relative to what it is in air, to prevent oxygen toxicity. The heliox mixture is what we all checked yesterday at the dive shop. In fact, we double checked each other's tanks for confirmation that all the mixes were good."

Bill motioned to the speaker and Mac to return to the dive platform. "Come on, you two, cut your jawing. We'll need a hand here."

Then Bill and Yvonne dropped into the water from the platform. In a cumbersome operation, they connected the body to the ship's winch, using canvas straps attached to the winch's cable. They motioned to Mac and Larsen's dive partner to winch the body up onto the dive platform.

By the time they managed to get the body and its associated equipment onto the boat and find a tarp to cover it, Sata-san surfaced.

"What's the verdict, Sata-san?"

"It is not clear. His mask was off when I find him. It seem he try to fix some trouble with it."

"Panic attack, yeah?" remarked Bill.

Mac was not comfortable with this diagnosis. He was confident that panic had no place in Larsen's repertoire of behavior patterns. Mac wondered what could have been the problem with Larsen's mask. It could have been an accident, but three dead scientists, in the same field of research, was reaching crowd status.

Toshimi arrived at the guest house just thirty minutes before he was due to meet Celeste and Mac and escort them to dinner at Tokushima's only surviving geisha house. He had been first upset, then disappointed, then disgruntled at the turn of events initiated by Larsen's death. Now that he had completed his obligations, he was at last able to execute a small part of his plan to host Celeste's first visit to Shikoku. He wished he didn't feel so exhausted.

It had taken two days to tidy up affairs in Ashizuri, making arrangements to transport the body and accommodating police procedures, while trying to keep as close as possible to the original travel plans of the conference participants. The burden, of course, had fallen on Toshimi. The dishonor of being responsible dictated his duty. And Toshimi was responsible, unless of course it had been murder, for which there was absolutely no evidence. Worsening his punishment was the fact that Toshimi had constructed an elaborate sight-seeing plan for Celeste and Mac. He planned to escort them to Tokushima by taking them the long way around the circumference of Shikoku. He was especially looking forward to taking them on the Yodo line, which crossed the mountains from Kubokawa Station to Uwajima, following the course of the Shimanto-gawa River. Not only is the line a masterful engineering accomplishment, but the scenery is some of the most beautiful in Japan. Celeste and Mac had shared the Bitterroot with him and now it was his turn to answer with the Shimanto-gawa. But this was not to be. Neither was he able to take them to Dogo Onsen, just outside of Matsuyama, where he had hoped to bathe with them in one of the most famous public baths in Japan, preserved in its original 1894 building.

Toshimi was profoundly grateful that he could count on Kazuko as if she were his own daughter. She had, of course, been more than willing to help out. At Toshimi's request, she changed her plans and accompanied Celeste and Mac on the Yodo line and then went as far as Matsuyama with them, where they did enjoy the baths. She put them on a train for Tokushima the following morning and then caught a flight back to Sapporo. Toshimi confirmed with the driver who collected him at the station that Celeste and Mac had arrived on schedule earlier in the afternoon and had checked in at the guest house. Having taken the more direct train route via Kochi, Toshimi could finally be reunited with his guests.

The Fukuda corporate guest house was located on a hill at the edge of a large park on the outskirts of Tokushima. It was an imposing four-story building, painted white, with twin curved roofs of green ceramic tile and red balustrades running around the outside of each upper floor. When Fukuda acquired its new vaccine production division on Shikoku, the guest house had been part of the deal. It had been built expressly for corporate retreats and for entertaining physicians who used the vaccine products of the original company. The Fukuda directors did not have similar patronage practices but they decided to maintain the building for their own meetings and to rent it out to other local businesses for small conferences.

Toshimi managed to wash, change his shirt, put on a fresh tie, and position himself at the bottom of the grand staircase just in time to greet Celeste and Mac as they descended for their rendezvous. He noted that the leather carpet slippers, for which guests exchanged their shoes at the door, did not fit either of them very well. They were both awkwardly trying not to slip on the carpeted stairs.

Having navigated the treacherous descent, Celeste planted a kiss on Toshimi's cheek, to the great amusement of the staff at the reception desk.

"How are you?" she asked. "Have things settled down?"

"Hai," said Toshimi flatly. "I am glad to be finished in Ashizuri. And very glad to be with you, at last. I hope that your trip has been good."

"Awesome," said Mac. "The Yodo line was incredible. It must go directly through at least half a dozen mountains."

"Hai," said Toshimi, this time with more enthusiasm. "It is close to knowing what it feels like to be a river. I am happy that you like it."

"I am sorry, though, that we did not take a bath together," said Celeste. "The bath at Dogo Onsen was excellent."

"Next time, next time," said Toshimi, pleased with the continuation of their joke. At least the visit would end well. "Our taxi waits and Araki-san would not like to wait more than he must to see his geisha."

The staff had arranged Toshimi's shoes next to Celeste's and Mac's. All of the toes were pointing to-

ward the door. The business of putting on shoes
suspended their conversation until they were inside
the taxi.

"Tell me about Araki-san and his geisha," said Celeste. She had devoured Arthur Golden's popular
novel, *Memoirs of a Geisha,* but hadn't realized that
the institution still existed. She did realize, however,
that if Mac hadn't been with her, she would never
have been treated to this experience.

"Masaki Araki is the head of our new vaccine division. He has been with Fukuda for a long time,
working at the main research laboratory in Osaka. His
specialty is the manufacture of pediatric formulations
and he has much experience with the world of pediatric medicine. He was an obvious choice for the head
of the vaccine division because most vaccines are
used by pediatricians. His wife is from Tokushima,
so she is happy to return here."

"I could never understand how a man can have a
wife and a geisha," said Mac.

"Ah," said Toshimi, "there are many ways to answer this. First, I should say I agree with you, because
there is nothing I enjoy more than the company of
my wife. But I am very lucky. Wives by tradition
were arranged. If you were very lucky, this could provide everything. But mostly there was a kind of division of labor."

"Like the man has the fun with the geisha and the
wife has the labor," said Mac.

"But it is more complicated than that. In this old
tradition, the wife had respectability and security and
the geisha did not. Geisha had to work hard for her
comfort. To make her desirable she had to excel in

artistic achievement. She had to be different from the wife. Anyway, now, the geisha is just a symbol of that tradition. She is employed by the restaurant to be special company at dinner. She is not supported by patrons anymore. Geisha house is not what it was. Now it is a place to enjoy tradition and part of tradition is to enjoy the company of a beautiful and accomplished woman."

"The sad part about that tradition is that it formalized the division between marriage and companionship," said Celeste. "But it was also, ironically, a tradition that respected intellectual and creative accomplishment by women, except that they weren't socially acceptable women."

"Given that argument, there is no place for a geisha house in modern society," said Mac.

"It is still a place where traditional music and dance are maintained," said Toshimi.

"Also," added Celeste, "I can even see a role for formalizing harmless flirtation outside of a marriage. Flirtation is highly restorative to self-esteem."

"Celeste!" exclaimed Mac, with horror. "I can't believe you're arguing in favor of an exploitative situation. Besides, how do you draw the line between flirtation and prostitution?"

Toshimi felt the tension crackle in the close air in the taxi. He quickly returned to the original subject. "Masaki Araki is a very special man. He likes Japanese tradition, but he also likes very modern things. He is an expert photographer. He made a beautiful calendar for Fukuda of photographs of his geisha in the kimino of different seasons. He is also an expert at many sports, especially golf and youeffokatcha."

"At what?" asked Celeste.

"Youeffokatcha," said Toshimi. He started to move his right arm in a mechanical way, making a humming noise, then dropped his hand from the elbow and made a grabbing gesture with his hand.

Presumably he was demonstrating "youeffokatcha" to Celeste, but she was absolutely clueless as to what he was illustrating. "Oh," she said politely.

While they had been discussing the morality of the geisha house, the taxi had moved from the boulevards into the small twisting streets of the restaurant district of Tokushima, which were decorated by festoons of lanterns. As Celeste was puzzling about further strategies to define youeffokatcha, the taxi pulled up in front of a building with sliding wooden doors and Toshimi set about paying the fare.

Out the window of the taxi, Celeste saw a tall man pacing back and forth in front of the restaurant entrance, sucking aggressively on a cigarette. He wore spectacles with heavy black frames and his wavy black hair was slicked back from his forehead. He was carrying a black satchel that looked like it might contain a camera and photography equipment. In the same hand, he was also carrying a plastic bag of the type dispensed at supermarkets. Catching sight of the taxi, he took a final drag, diminishing at least an inch of tobacco, and tossed the cigarette into the gutter. He waited by the curb while they climbed out of the taxi.

"Araki-san," said Toshimi, "this is Dr. Celeste Braun and her friend Mac." After they shook hands, Masaki Araki reached into his plastic bag and withdrew two small stuffed toys. He presented one to Celeste and one to Mac.

"I have good luck at youeffokatcha while I am waiting. Here is a souvenir of Japan." He grinned proudly.

Celeste and Mac politely inspected the toys. They were pandalike and doglike creatures with round eyes and wings. They looked to be comic book characters, possibly Pokémon-derived; Celeste wasn't sure. Her puzzlement increased.

"Thank you very much," she said, trying to admire her toy with conviction. "This will be a nice souvenir."

"You are most welcome," said Araki-san graciously. "And now we should enter." He gestured to the wooden doors, which slid open and revealed a row of three geisha girls and their mama-san all bowing and smiling.

As Celeste and Mac entered they were greeted by a chorus of "Welcome, Dr. Celeste Braun and Mac," accompanied by much giggling.

The four guests removed their shoes at the door and were led up the carpeted stairs by the mama-san, entering a *tatami* room with a large low table, beautifully laid out. Three men in business suits were already seated cross-legged at the table. The geishas followed them into the room.

The men were introduced as scientists from the research division. As the third man was introduced, Toshimi whispered to Celeste that he was a rival with Araki-san for his geisha.

Celeste and Mac were seated next to each other in the center of one side of the long table. Masaki Araki and Toshimi sat across from them and the other men spread themselves around. Araki introduced the geishas, Fumiko, Yuriko, and Satsu. They were wearing identical elaborate kimonos in colors of pale peach. Though they looked quite young even under their heavy white makeup, they were extremely poised.

Fumiko, evidently the target of the rivalry between Araki-san and his colleague, knelt behind Celeste and Mac. "We have been looking forward to your visit, Dr. Celeste Braun," she said in perfect English. "We are also happy to meet Mac. My sisters say he looks like an American movie star." She smiled mischievously. All the girls giggled. Then Fumiko took orders for drinks.

The dinner unfolded with dish after exquisite dish, each presented in special receptacles with additional elaborate holders for sauces and accompaniments. Celeste guessed that they would use hundreds of individual pieces of crockery by the end of the meal. The contents of each dish was explained by mama-san or one of the geishas. When explanations were not obvious, mama-san consulted a calculator-sized translation computer, which was stowed inside the layers of her kimono. While this was not terribly useful, it certainly provided additional entertainment. Celeste was compelled to define *smooching,* a word produced by the computer to name a certain fish they were eating. The following day she would discover that her definition had lost something in translation when Toshimi introduced her as a "smooching" friend at the beginning of her lecture.

Celeste was impressed by how much the girls were in control of the evening. It was hardly the exploitative situation imagined by Mac. The girls' English was superior to that of the men from Fukuda, presumably because the younger generation were more influenced by globalization. The geishas kept the alcohol flowing and flirted gracefully, performing a single traditional dance, which was quite chaste and poignant. They took their performance very seriously and made Celeste think more of earnest schoolgirls than of clever prostitutes. Araki-san, having set up his camera, gave imperious instructions for lighting the dance properly to his more junior "rival." If anyone was being exploited, it seemed to Celeste that it was the men whose vanity was being flattered while their pocketbooks were being depleted.

Several times during the meal the group was joined by other men, apparently making the rounds of the several dinners taking place in the same restaurant. The visitors would take a seat at the end of the table, order some sake, and chat over it for a half hour or so. Celeste had the sense that she and Mac were being inspected like bizarre curios. Considerable anticipation of Celeste's lecture the following day was expressed and many business cards were exchanged.

Toward the end of the evening, while they were finishing up the sake, they had a visit from the head of the virus vaccine section. Both Celeste and Mac had recently met him in Ashizuri. He was an urbane scientist who had spent several years at a cancer research laboratory in Houston. He had been on the fateful boat trip at the end of the conference and raised the subject that had been noticeably avoided all evening.

Masaki Araki wanted to hear the details.

"I have done that dive," he announced. "It is a goal

for deep divers of Shikoku. What was the body like?"

Mac was a little taken aback by the question. He'd had a good look at Larsen's body when they had dragged it up on deck. "Well, his mask was off, of course still attached to the regulator line. And he had some funny marks on his face, like bite marks. Also, he was sort of twisted. Like he'd had a convulsion."

"Ah," said Araki-san. "I am guessing it is the same as what happen to Omoto. Omoto die of oxygen toxicity. He was sick in his mask and remove it to clear it. Then he lose control. When I find him, fish are cleaning his face and mask. It was very sad. Omoto make mistake to measure his oxygen. It was too high."

"No, that can't be it," said Mac. "Larsen's buddy saw him switch to the lower oxygen tank and he confirmed that the switch was successful. The tanks were checked by two people at least, so it's unlikely a mistake was made in measuring the oxygen content."

"Then someone change his label to another tank," said Araki-san with conviction. "Police will check tank oxygen content. They will also find the regulator blocked from when he was sick."

No one stated the obvious implication, but Toshimi said, "Excuse me, I think I will call investigator right away." He left the room quickly with his cell phone in hand.

The party broke up as soon as Toshimi returned. He had managed to get through to the investigator, who assured Toshimi that these facts would be known in the morning.

Mama-san and the geishas bowed them out with ceremony. Celeste wondered fleetingly if any of the men would return for a more private party, but she was reasonably convinced she had seen the sum total of what a modern geisha house was all about.

Out on the street, Araki-san immediately lit up a cigarette. "Youeffokatcha," he said with glee. "Come with me."

They followed him down the crowded street, past groups of men in suits with loosened ties, on their way home from business dinners. About halfway down the block, Araki-san stopped in front of a video game arcade flashing with neon lights. He stood reverentially in front of a glass booth facing onto the street. It was filled with stuffed toys, with a metal claw suspended over them. The claw was decorated like a spaceship or, Celeste realized, an unidentified flying object, the mysterious "you-eff-o." A lighted sign at the top of the booth confirmed her revelation, indicating that this was the game of UFO Catcher.

"I am expert," said Araki-san. And indeed, for each one hundred yen piece he was provided to feed the machine, he manipulated the UFO to capture a toy, loading them up with more souvenirs.

In keeping with his reputation as a sportsman, Araki-san also proved to be an expert in diving matters. The following morning, just after Celeste delivered her lecture at the Fukuda lecture hall, To-shimi received a call from the police in Ashizuri. The contents of the tank that was labeled as low-oxygen heliox, with Lars Larsen's name on the red tag, was identical to the contents of the high oxygen nitrox for the certified shallow divers. The only con-clusion that could be drawn was the one that Araki-

san had intimated. Someone must have switched
Larsen's name label to a nitrox tank, after he had
checked his tank at the dive shop, at some time before
the dive.

10

Publish or Perish

Celeste straightened up from her hunched position at the computer. She was finalizing the text of the manuscript that she and Karen were about to send off. They had been working on it steadily since Celeste's return from Japan a week earlier. Searching for just the right turn of phrase, Celeste stretched her arms to the ceiling, while dropping her shoulder blades, to loosen the tension between them. She considered this the "shrubbery" pose. It mimicked the upper half of the yoga tree position. Her gaze was drawn down the westward streets of the Sunset district fifteen floors below, to the Pacific Ocean, serenely spreading to the horizon from its neat seam of white breakers along Ocean Beach. Celeste began to think about the submission cover letter she would need to write, which led her to worry about the publication outcome, her impending tenure evaluation, and then, as was inevitable in the past week, her thoughts turned to the demise of her senior colleagues.

Celeste had now lost three of the referees who had been asked to write on her behalf for her tenure promotion. The entire shadow cabinet had lost their husbands. One husband was apparently murdered and the other two had succumbed to strange accidents. All the deaths were related to their nonscientific pursuits, in which they claimed expertise. Celeste couldn't help recalling her brief conversation with Inspector Charron in Vendée. Would he speculate that these deaths were merely the price of vanity or that they were the vengeance of a jealous academic or both? Just as likely they could be the result of nefarious activity of the hypothetical bioblaster, targeting high-placed scientists for any number of reasons. However, this latter theory still seemed to Celeste to be ridiculously paranoid, a fabrication from European images of a crazed America. Besides, there was no evidence whatsoever that two of the deaths were anything but accidental.

Celeste forced herself to focus on the task at hand. The fact that she was thrilled about the science that she was in the process of reporting made it considerably easier. The cell sorter experiments that Celeste had suggested to Karen had provided the breakthrough they needed. Based on this data, Karen could confidently say that the gene she had cloned was distinct from the gene identified by Rank and Dyer, and that both genes controlled independent strategies for a virus to evade the immune response. Karen had also solidly established the location of five similar genes and now they knew that one was identical to that reported by Rank. Karen's work was beautifully executed and Celeste found it satisfying that Rank's findings were complementary, lending more significance to the breakthrough. Evidently the virus had evolved multiple tactics for achieving the same result, presumably for dealing with variation in the human immune system. Celeste concluded the manuscript by discussing the phenomenon in terms of the inevitable evolutionary interplay between the host and the pathogen. It was also important to point out that the products of the viral genes they had identified would merit consideration as targets in the development of antiviral therapy.

Ironically, to maximize the impact of the work from Celeste's lab, it was critical that Rank's paper be published close to the same time. The joint results were likely to cause quite a stir in the scientific community. This was where the submission cover letter would play a key role in the process. Celeste needed to inform the editor of the journal to which she was submitting the manuscript about the existence of Rank's work. The editor would then contact Rank to find out whether his work was under review or already in press. Then, if Celeste's paper was found acceptable, the journal would try to coordinate the publication date with that of Rank's paper and would possibly publish an accompanying analytical piece summarizing the significance of the two papers. There were so many ifs in the whole process, and Celeste's anxiety level responded accordingly as she considered each one. On the positive side, the work seemed so remarkably coherent. Could she even dare to be hopeful?

When Celeste finished drafting the cover letter, she printed out a copy and a copy of the manuscript text and went to look for Karen. She found her in the departmental computer room printing out the latest data figures for the manuscript. They exchanged the segments each had been working on for final comments and approval. Three hours later, the whole thing was finished and the four copies for submission were bundled up with the cover letter. Karen walked the package down to the Federal Express drop box.

Celeste returned to her office feeling satisfied with the manuscript, but also drained. She had put off dealing with routine paperwork and most of her e-mail during the intense week of manuscript preparation and her desk was covered with stacks of things that needed attention. Long experience told her that it would be better to wait until morning to begin to tackle this kind of backlog. But she decided to listen to today's phone messages, which she had also ignored in the final push to get the paper out, just in case there was something urgent.

There was, in fact. It was an issue that Celeste had, with Freudian amnesia, completely forgotten. The real estate agent certainly hadn't. The three messages in sequence betrayed the agent's increasing annoyance that she hadn't yet heard from Celeste. The final message stated quite clearly that if Celeste wanted to maintain her interest in purchasing the other unit in her building, she would need to get her bid on paper by the end of the day. Celeste had no time to dither or to think about Mac. She phoned the agent immediately to say she would be right over. After all, the first bid was only to stay in the running.

The fate of Celeste's manuscript and her real estate offer were still unresolved almost two weeks later, when the Utah medical examiner, Dr. Hyman Lockwood, found himself waiting impatiently in the swank lobby of the ski resort hotel at Snowbird. As he looked around at the indoor waterfall and fountain and the slick black marble décor, he wished that Baker had been able to accompany him. Dealing with the snow crowd was not the favorite part of his job. It wasn't as though he hadn't done his time on the slopes. On the contrary, he had been quite a good skier. But one day at the height of the season, almost twenty years ago now, he had just gone off the whole business. He was standing at the top of a run and was suddenly struck by the idiocy of the activity, with its accompanying hype, the fancy outfits, the incessant waiting on line, the posturing, and the high turkey factor among skiers. He completed that run and retired his downhill skis forever. Living in Utah, of course, provided him plenty of good cross-country opportunities and he still happily plowed the trails in peace and quiet, stopping to smoke the occasional cigar and take in the scenery.

Now Lockwood had to shift his mentality back to the downhill world. He wasn't going to get his hopes up for the interview. At least there was no significant snow left in the area, this late in June, so he wouldn't have to talk about the day's run. It was the disappearance of the snow that had prompted the interview in the first place, since this was the time when the lost skis were rounded up and sorted for return to the various rental outfits in the area.

Mike Nolan approached him, striding across the lobby. He was wearing faded blue jeans and a black rugby shirt with a white collar. He looked exactly how Lockwood imagined a deep-powder ski guide would look, rugged and clean-shaven with long blond hair. Nolan had no trouble identifying Lockwood either, who looked exactly how he imagined the state medical examiner would look.

Lockwood was pleasantly surprised, however, at Nolan's New Zealand accent. At least he was dealing with a cosmopolitan airhead.

"All right, Nolan," said Lockwood, after they had introduced themselves. "I'm here because you contacted the local police regarding a ski accident on one of your powder trips. I think you'd better take it from the top."

"Yeah, sure," obliged Nolan. "This past February there was a fatal accident on one of my trips. The guy lost his ski as soon as he dropped from the chopper and went out of control. He ran into a tree. I remembered that he had the latest model Salomon skis 'cause I was thinking about trying a demo pair myself and we talked about it. So it wasn't hard to recognize the ski when it came back to our shop after the meltdown roundup. It had our label on it 'cause we check the adjustments of all the skis with the clients present, just to be extra sure that nothing can go wrong once we're in the powder. I saw straight away that the binding had been tampered with. I guess I was also kinda looking out for something, 'cause that accident shouldn't have happened."

"After the bindings were checked, where were the skis stored?"

"They were in my private locker, at the launching pad. We take them there directly from the shop to be ready for liftoff."

"Could anyone have had access to that locker?"

"I suppose they could have. It's not locked, since

the launch site is locked. I'm normally at the launch site early to open it up, but I didn't open up that day. In fact, I was almost late for the trip."

"I'm impressed that you remember that detail," said Lockwood. Perhaps he was dealing with someone more intelligent than he'd anticipated.

"Well, you'd have remembered her, too," sighed Nolan. "It was tough to get out of bed."

"So I take it that you were, uh, distracted, the whole night before the trip as well."

"That's one way to put it."

"Hmmph. Sounds like there was plenty of opportunity for tampering then. I don't suppose you remember your partner's name?"

"Carol," said Nolan.

"That it?"

"She was a married woman," he explained.

"Great," acknowledged Lockwood flatly. "Can you remember who was around at the time of the launch?"

"No one unusual, just the people going on the trip and the chopper mechanic, who I guess let them into the launch site. And, oh yeah, the boyfriend of one of the girls going up with us was there. He wasn't too keen on her going. He had no need to worry. She'd practically been born on skis."

"Do you remember anyone else, specifically?"

"No, can't say that I do. The reporter asked me the same question and I've been working on it ever since. But no luck."

"You spoke to a reporter about this?" Lockwood could hardly contain himself.

"Sure," said Nolan. "We don't want our trips to get a bad rap. So if there's murder involved, it's not our fault. We've gotta set the story straight."

Lockwood did not believe for a minute that a straight story would emerge once the newspapers got hold of it. He raised his eyebrows. "It's no good telling you now that you should have kept quiet about it while we investigate." Lockwood was keenly aware of his erroneous assumption. There was no hint of intelligence at work here. He sighed with resignation.

The following morning, at the office in Salt Lake City, Baker made a pot of coffee as usual and laid out the national and local newspapers on Lockwood's desk. Tidying the medical records room, a task Baker had postponed for months, seemed suddenly like an excellent idea. It would give Lockwood some time to digest the headlines. Baker correctly surmised that Lockwood would not be thrilled to learn that the "bioblaster" conspiracy against a group of virologists was now front-page news from New York to San Francisco. Evidently the announcement that George Churchill's ski accident was not accidental had all but confirmed the existence of a nefarious perpetrator.

Ivan Rank was often angry but rarely frightened. The morning the bioblaster story appeared, he felt so terrified that he was afraid to leave his house to go into the laboratory. In desperation, he phoned Wally Dyer. Without explicitly stating his concern, Rank asked Wally to drop by on his way in to work. They'd been very careful about appearances and assiduously avoided coming in to work together, should their friendship be misconstrued. But now it would be understood that if Wally were staying with Rank it was for protection against the bioblaster. And nobody could object to that. After all, Rank's huge rambling house near Rittenhouse Square could easily hold two and there was no question that it was a scary place to be stalked.

Rank paced restlessly around the rooms of the ground floor while he awaited Wally's arrival. The antique furniture he had inherited from his grandmother creaked in protest at his nervous perambulation and the strings of his grand piano resonated with an eerie, hollow sound. When the doorbell finally rang, Rank checked through the peephole before he opened the front door. He was reassured simply by the sight of Wally's fresh face and confident expression. If he had been a woman, he would have fallen into Wally's arms for a comforting hug as soon as he opened the door. But as it was, he ushered Wally furtively inside and closed the door quickly. He touched Wally very briefly on the arm to direct him into the kitchen. Rank saw his own hand tremble visibly as he reached out in this simple gesture.

"Thank you for coming, dear boy," said Rank. "The least I can do is make you a cappuccino. Then I need your advice."

"Don't worry, Ivan. It's no trouble at all."

Rank fussed with the cappuccino maker while Wally made himself comfortable at the kitchen table, lounging with the ease of familiarity. When it looked as though Rank had things under way, Wally asked, "What's up, Ivan?"

"Did you see the paper this morning?"

"Not yet. You know I usually just catch up by reading yours on Sunday morning."

Rank spread the front page out before Wally on the

table. "I'm sure she's doing it. She's got to be the bioblaster. All these deaths in our field. It's no coincidence that they were supposed to be writing letters about her tenure promotion." His words caught in his throat before he could articulate his real fear. "I'm sure I'm next," he said in a small, anxious voice.

Wally was worried to see Rank so worked up. It wasn't that his mentor was showing weakness. That he could deal with. It made him feel needed. After all, relationships were built on give and take. But he was genuinely afraid for Rank's health. Wally knew only too well how fragile Rank's emotional stability was.

"Come sit, Ivan," said Wally, patting the seat beside him. Rank obeyed, childlike. Even sitting, Wally was a head taller than Rank, who was beginning to wizen with age. Wally was also reasonably fit and well built. He reached out a slender, muscular arm and firmly rested his hand on Rank's shoulder. "We can stop her," he said with assurance. "And for as long as you're worried, I'll stay here. I know you've got plenty of room for me."

Rank simultaneously melted and gained strength at Wally's touch. He reached up to Wally's hand and covered it with his own, patting it gently. "I knew I could count on you, dear boy. I feel better already. Now, how do you propose we stop her?"

"Let's talk about it after you've relaxed a bit. Shall we work a little on that duet we started last week?"

"That would be delightful," said Rank, breathing a contented sigh of relief.

11

Snail's Pace

It was the morning after the bioblaster story broke. Celeste was in her office unusually early, trying to make headway through the administrative backlog that had steadily accumulated while she was on the road and then working on Karen's manuscript. Procrastinating from dealing with the bottomless piles on her desk, Celeste checked her e-mail and was pleased to see Harry Freeman's name appear. She hadn't heard from him since receiving the plaintive letter that had disturbed her on the eve of leaving for Japan. She had written from Japan what she hoped was a conciliatory answer, reassuring Harry that his friendship was a fundamental part of her life. She had tried to explain that her relationship with Mac didn't change that in any way. Harry's subsequent silence, for almost a month, had worried her and she was understandably anxious to see what he had to say.

"Your letter was much appreciated," began the message. "Should you need me, I'm still here. Now for more immediate concerns. It seems the French police may have had the right hunch after all. Any ideas about the perpetrator? Why clean out this field in particular? What's to gain from the vacancies? These questions are not just reporter's curiosity. You could be at risk. Be careful. As ever, Harry."

Though terse, the first two sentences and the "as ever" generated a pang of nostalgia for Harry's embrace. It seemed he was still hurting and Celeste doubted that he would have written had he not been concerned about the bioblaster and whether Celeste might be targeted. If there was such a lunatic out there, it certainly wasn't out of the question that Celeste could be on the hit list. Celeste continued to feel, however, that the bioblaster idea was highly preposterous. The very focused attack on senior members of a small field suggested some knowledge of the field. In contrast, someone like the Unabomber would be likely to attack a broader group of people with more public visibility. Besides, the Unabomber had a political agenda against technology. A political agenda for attacks on virologists was hard to justify, given that their research is so relevant to human health. If the deaths of Churchill and Larsen were the act of one person, and Pogue's death did turn out to be murder by the same hand, Celeste felt the perpetrator was more likely to be someone associated with the field. Of course, this thought wasn't particularly reassuring, since Celeste had no idea whether she might share the characteristics of her late senior colleagues that qualified them for elimination.

Imagining potential perpetrators in the field, Celeste resuscitated a speculation that had begun as a joke with Mac, but now seemed considerably less amusing. Someone like Dot Grantham could certainly benefit in a number of ways if the field were cleared. Celeste would be bereft of tenure supporters and Grantham could build strength in the field in her new department, with little competition from elsewhere. Celeste's consideration of Grantham's overt ambition replaced her own nervousness about the situation with sufficient irritation that she was provoked to begin a response. "Dear Harry," Celeste wrote, "Since you asked, one person who has everything to gain is my current chair." Then she thought better of it. Apparently e-mail messages never really disappeared from the system and such a statement would be considered legally slanderous. She deleted the sentence and started over, but was interrupted by the telephone. It was the provost's secretary with an unprecedented summons. Celeste was requested to appear in the provost's office, immediately, to help out with an urgent situation.

Celeste knew the provost fairly well. Before he became provost, he and Celeste had taught together in one of the medical school courses. They had spent many hours jointly adapting medical case reports to use as teaching material and Celeste had found his company pleasant and educational. Celeste wasn't exactly in the provost's inner circle of faculty advisors, though. In fact, she hadn't been in his office since he had moved into the administrative compound, almost two years earlier. In this new office, Celeste did not have to clear a pile of papers onto the floor in order to sit down in the chair opposite the desk. It seemed that signs of scholarly work correlated inversely with administrative power, at least at BAU.

The provost was a clean-shaven, dapper man in his early sixties and was almost completely bald. In his teaching days he was always well turned out in a tie and V-neck sweater and in combination with his horn-rimmed glasses he looked like the quintessential medical school professor. This attire had now been replaced by a suit. While his spectacles were a more trendy design, his face was considerably more careworn than when he and Celeste had worked on their class together.

"It's good to see you, Celeste," said the provost. "Though I wish it were under different circumstances."

Celeste's uneasiness escalated. She had never heard of tenure decisions being announced by the provost, but maybe it was a new policy.

"I'll get straight to the point," he continued. "We've received some disturbing allegations about you that have upset your chair enormously. She came to see me a few minutes ago. Apparently she received a communication suggesting that you might be involved in these terrible tragedies that have struck in your field. The implication was that you had arranged to eliminate those who would not write favorable letters for your promotion."

"Who from?" Celeste was flabbergasted.

"I'm really not at liberty to say. However, I must say, immediately, that I find this ridiculous. The problem is that these accusations may become public."

"That would be slander," pointed out Celeste, conscious of the irony.

"Of course it would be," said the provost. "But we can't afford any kind of negative publicity just now.

The financing for the Hidden Point project is shaky as it is. If we can't get the last ten million by the end of this month, then we won't make the contract deadline with the city for leasing the land. Then the whole thing will have to be renegotiated from the beginning. There's so much neighborhood opposition to the building that it may not go through a second time."

"That's less than a week from now."

"That's right." The provost sighed. The tension showed in the tightening wrinkles whose outlines were already etched on his brow.

Celeste's thoughts were churning, reeling from the accusation reported by Grantham and its consequences. Celeste herself could be a potential murder victim, yet she was suddenly being put in the position not only of defending her own innocence but of having to save a campus endeavor that she considered fruitless from the start. She was outraged and at the same time cruelly denied any protection.

Celeste was not thinking clearly while these reactions percolated. Responding to the superficial issue, she said the first thing that came into her head to address the provost's concerns. "Maybe it would be a boon to the campus if Hidden Point fell through."

"Pardon me," said the provost, in disbelief.

There was no turning back. Celeste's sense of panic and abandonment stimulated her to persist in saying what she thought. Besides, it seemed to Celeste that the provost was more concerned about bad publicity than he was about Celeste's complicity in murder. This realization fueled a momentary and foolish rebellion. "The move to Hidden Point is going to cause logistical and scientific nightmares," replied Celeste.

"All kinds of cross-disciplinary programs are going to be split. And these are the programs from which our campus has made its academic reputation."

"You know, Celeste, I'm well aware of that. But if we want to grow, we will have to change. I'm surprised to hear such a conservative opinion from a junior faculty member."

"Maybe I am conservative. But another way to look at it is if it ain't broke, don't fix it."

"Many faculty feel that the lack of space is entirely constraining. This is a problem that does need fixing."

"Constraining perhaps to their personal power base," responded Celeste.

The provost raised his eyebrows. "I am here to serve the needs of my faculty," he said. "The grass-roots push from our long-term members has been overwhelmingly in favor of the campus split. They have volunteered to be the first to move. If this is their desire, then I support them. If it doesn't go through, then a lot of promises will have to be broken."

Celeste could just imagine who the disappointed faculty would be. She doubted that any of them were untenured. She also understood with sudden clarity that the provost was merely a pawn of these powerful faculty members. There was absolutely no point in arguing with him. The only recourse she had was to work on clearing her own name, so that if the funding of Hidden Point failed, it couldn't be blamed on her. Certainly this was a prerequisite to saving whatever slim chance she now had of promotion.

"I sympathize with your position," she conceded, lamely. "I definitely don't want to be the cause of the failure of the Hidden Point scheme because of negative publicity for the campus. What do you think I should do about this accusation?"

"The only thing that would help would be identification of the real murderer."

"That's assuming that the same person killed both Churchill and Larsen."

"Isn't there a third victim?"

"Richard Pogue also died at a recent conference in France, but there's no evidence that his death wasn't an accident of food poisoning and bad timing."

"It is suspicious, though," said the provost. "This article, describing all three deaths, was sent along with the letter to Grantham. In fact, it was the death in France that led to the theory that American scientists are being threatened by a so-called bioblaster."

"May I see it?" asked Celeste.

The provost handed over the newspaper article. There was a small front-page paragraph stapled to a full back page, with several articles devoted to the situation. Photographs of all three deceased scientists were reproduced at the top of the inside page. There was also a photograph of the ski guide who had discovered that Churchill's ski had been tampered with and an account of an interview with the guide. The caption under his photograph said, "Otherwise engaged." Celeste noted that the story came from the *Philadelphia Inquirer*. Given the source of the article, there was only one person who could have written to Grantham. The accusation had to be coming from Ivan Rank.

"I understand," said Celeste to the provost. "If

there's anything I can do to clear my name, I will."
She sounded more confident than she felt.

Celeste returned to her office and tried to consider
the situation rationally. She could only hope that
scientific reasoning would help her see a pattern, as
it had in her past brushes with the criminal world.
Although the work from her lab was going better
than ever, she was steadily losing confidence in her
ability to apply scientific rationale to her personal
problems.

If Ivan Rank were rational, which Celeste knew
was not the case, he would have realized that Celeste
had not even been present when the first murder had
occurred. She supposed he could make the argument
that she had worked with an accomplice. So if she
had an accomplice, who was a likely candidate? Mac
had been at all three conferences. So had many other
scientists in the field. But then, the accomplice would
have to have a motive, as compelling as Rank believed Celeste's was, to agree to collaborate. If there
were someone with an equally strong motive, then
why implicate Celeste at all? It was obvious that Rank
had not thought it through. The first thing to do was
to make a list of all the people who had attended all
three conferences. Celeste had the participant lists for
the two conferences she had attended. It didn't take
her long to check the overlap. It wasn't anywhere near
as extensive as she had suspected. She knew Mac had
a participant list from the ski meeting because she had
already asked him about Rank's abstract from the
meeting program. Fortunately, she got through to him

on the phone in his lab and explained briefly what was going on.

"I can fax you the list, no problem," replied Mac. "But I think you're wasting your time. I'll probably wind up as your prime suspect. Of course, then you'd have to interrogate me, so I wouldn't mind."

"Mac, this is serious," said Celeste.

"All right, if it's serious, then I say, *'Cherchez la femme!'* "

"Just send the list," Celeste said and hung up the phone.

She was not amused, but Mac's remark—a reference to the classic French detective fiction strategy, translated as "look for the woman (or wife)"—reminded Celeste of the fictional Inspector Maigret, and then of the very real Inspector Charron. He had been, as the French say, *très sympathique*. Perhaps he could help.

Checking her watch, Celeste saw that it was only eleven. There was a chance that, if Charron were working late, he might be reached in his office. And he had definitely seemed like the type to work late. Celeste returned to the pile of papers from which she had just extracted the list of participants from the meeting in Vendée. She located other papers from the meeting and with them, she found Charron's business card. Celeste tapped out the number and waited.

"Allô? Ici l'inspecteur Charron."

"Hello, Monsieur Charron, this is Celeste Braun from Bay Area University. We met in Vendée at the conference where Richard Pogue died."

"*Ah, oui.* The young woman. What can I do for you, mademoiselle?"

Celeste described the situation regarding the accusation and the threat to her promotion. She finished by saying, "I thought that maybe you might have some information about Pogue's death, that could help me figure out if someone is actually responsible for all three deaths. The bioblaster theory seems to be coming from France and suggests that all three men were murdered."

"*Quelle barbe,*" said Charron in reply to Celeste's monologue. Her French was good enough to understand that Charron was essentially saying "what a mess." "This bioblaster theory has taken a life of its own," explained Charron. "It was a private theory, which was seized by the press, with no strong evidence. I did tell them that it was a *fantaisie.*"

"You mean you have no evidence that Pogue was murdered?"

"No. It is extremely annoying. We test the snails, as the young doctor suggest. Yes, here is the analysis." Celeste could hear Charron rustling paper on his desk. "*Quarante-huit escargots. Normaux.*"

"That's forty-eight normal snails?"

"*Exactement.*"

Celeste was silent for a moment. "I think," she said slowly, "that there were forty-nine snails. I believe that Richard Pogue had an extra one on his plate and there should have been eight of us at the head table. Let me see . . . Mac and me, the Pogues, the Larsens, Antoine Suchet, and Claude. So that would make forty-eight plus one extra."

"Are you absolutely positive?"

"Well, I know someone I can ask for confirmation," said Celeste. "Would it make a difference?

"Of course, mademoiselle. If it was not an error in your count or ours, someone could have taken a snail for a reason. If it had poison, for example."

"I'll get back to you right away," said Celeste. "Will you be there?"

"I must go to dine soon. If I am not here, you can leave me a message. I will be at work tomorrow."

"Saturday?"

"But of course, mademoiselle."

"Maybe this is it," said Celeste hopefully.

"We shall see," said Charron. *"Au revoir. Et merci, mademoiselle."*

"You're welcome," said Celeste.

Celeste didn't even replace the receiver. She terminated the connection by hand and dialed Mac's number in the lab. She got through to one of the fellows who worked with him.

"Mac's gone for the weekend," he said. "Who did you say this was?"

"Celeste Braun."

"Okay," said the voice on the line. "Mac said that if you called, you should check your e-mail."

"Thanks," said Celeste, wondering what was going on, as she hung up the phone.

Turning to her computer, Celeste checked the mail for the second time that day and opened a new message from Mac.

"I was feeling like the character in *The Mikado* who has a 'little list.' I decided to bring it to you in person. Will arrive by standby this evening. Can't wait to see you. Love, Mac."

Celeste would have to wait for resolution.

• • •

Dot Grantham sat at the desk in her office looking blankly at the letter she had received from Ivan Rank, which still lay on the artificial leather blotter. She was unnerved by the provost's reaction to the news about Celeste Braun. Grantham hadn't realized that funding for the Hidden Point project was so tenuous. She pondered the consequences of its failure and was not happy about losing her prospects of power.

Surely there must be sources of funding that were yet untapped, Grantham mused.

Rank's letter materialized in Grantham's line of focus. It seemed to tremble with the vitriol it conveyed. Rank himself was known for his ability to fund his research with large donations from the vaccine industry. Perhaps he would be willing to divulge a contact who might be interested in investment at Hidden Point or at least in a donation to BAU. Grantham would, of course, make it clear that she and Rank had a mutual interest as far as Celeste Braun was concerned. It certainly wouldn't do any harm to give him a call.

Rank must have been screening his calls. As Dot Grantham identified herself to the message machine, the connection clicked and Rank spoke. "Hello, Ivan Rank here."

"Hello, Ivan. This is Dot Grantham from BAU. How are you?"

"Rather uncomfortable with this bioblaster business unsolved." His voice was cranky.

"Yes, I'm sure. That was what I was phoning about. I received your letter and wanted to reassure you that I have taken it to the very top. We obviously need to do something about Celeste Braun immediately."

"That's an understatement," said Rank, only slightly more agreeably.

"Unfortunately our provost is worried that the negative publicity might jeopardize funding for our expansion at Hidden Point. I've heard from Wally Dyer and others how successful you've been in attracting investment in your own department. I was wondering if you could suggest some industrial contacts we could approach to help make the situation more secure. It would be a shame if justice were not done for political reasons." Rank's extravagant recruitment of Wally Dyer to his department was common knowledge and Grantham thought that invoking Dyer's name might help her case.

"I doubt that the contacts I have would be interested in investment in a new campus. They're more oriented toward vaccine development," whined Rank.

It was obvious to Grantham that Rank was grasping at excuses. She needed to remind him of her power over Celeste Braun.

"Well, I'm looking for support for expansion of the virology effort in my new department. An infusion of funds here at the Olympus site would free up other funds for Hidden Point. You realize," continued Grantham pointedly, "that with the opening left by Dr. Braun, I'll have at least three new positions to fill."

"Wally Dyer's only just come here. I'm sure he's not interested in moving elsewhere," said Rank irritably. Who did she think she was, trying to raid his department for money and personnel? "If your provost won't move on the Braun issue, the newspapers will see that justice is done."

"Ivan, I'm afraid you've completely misunderstood me," said Grantham, trying to salvage the situation. "I'm doing my best for our mutual interest and was hoping for a little support."

"You've got my support," said Rank stubbornly.

To herself, Grantham admitted defeat, and hung up as gracefully as she could under the circumstances.

Ivan Rank glowered at the telephone. Could he really be so confident about Wally's loyalty? Was this woman trying to steal his star faculty member from under his nose? He could feel his blood pressure rising. There was only one way to answer his dilemma.

Moments later, Wally Dyer looked up at Ivan Rank, who stood in the doorway. Rank's expression was frightful.

"Ivan, what is it?"

"I didn't know you knew Dot Grantham."

"Well, I don't really. I think I met her a couple of years ago, at a meeting, right before I came here. I know who she is, of course, from when we were working on your letter."

"You mean she hasn't been trying to hire you for her new department?"

"Heavens, no. Whatever gave you that idea? You know I'm very happy here. And I would never leave you."

"Ah, dear boy," said Ivan. "I've just heard some nasty gossip. Didn't believe a word of it, of course. Please forgive me."

"Now, Ivan," said Wally solicitously, looking at his watch. "You know it's not good to worry on an empty stomach. I've been wanting to try that new sushi place down the street. Would you like to join me?"

"I'd like nothing more, dear boy."

12

Name Game

Inspector Charron had been obliged to run errands for Madame Charron while the Saturday market still had some momentum, so had been forced to postpone his arrival at the office until late morning. Finally, after listening twice to the voice-mail message from the American woman, he sat back in his desk chair and lit his pipe. His thoughts on the Pogue case needed stimulation. Apparently, Celeste Braun had checked with her fiancé, the previous evening, and they both agreed that they remembered an extra snail on Richard Pogue's plate. Charron recollected that they were a thoughtful couple and he had no reason to doubt their powers of observation. They were scientists, after all.

He sucked on the stem of his pipe and released the smoke with a sigh. A missing snail could suggest that someone removed it to eliminate evidence of poisoning, as Charron had intimated to Celeste during their earlier conversation. Alternatively, the collection of snail shells for analysis could have been careless and one shell might have been left behind inadvertently.

But assuming that a poisoned snail *was* the cause of Pogue's death, the murderer would have needed an accomplice to block the bridge from Noirmoutier to the mainland. Certainly, the first thing that would have been done at the mainland hospital would have been to pump Pogue's stomach and he might have survived had he been still alive upon arrival.

For what seemed to be at least the hundredth time, Charron looked over the file on the case. He hadn't paid much attention to the information on the bridge accident because it hadn't seemed significant. Now he was able to look at it in a new light. And, much to Charron's satisfaction, it appeared there might be something to pursue there after all. Consulting the clock on his desk, he realized it was too early to telephone Celeste Braun. She had left a home telephone number, but he did not have the heart to wake her, and presumably her fiancé, at what would be three A.M. in San Francisco. He would have to phone after his lunch. Madame Charron would not be pleased.

Mac was not particularly pleased either, when the phone next to Celeste's bed rang at seven A.M. on Saturday morning. As Celeste reached for the phone, her naked body brushed against the insistent erection with which he had awakened. His cock seemed to defy the fact that it had expended itself forcefully during the previous night's lovemaking. It certainly didn't understand why she didn't just let the answering machine pick up.

"Hello?" said Celeste, sleepily.

"Ah, *excusez-moi,*" said Charron. "I am sorry if I wake you. This is Charron. Shall I call later?"

"No, no, it's fine. Did you get my message?"

"Yes, but I do not know how much it can tell us. However, there is one new thing that I begin to think about. If there was a poisoned snail, then someone must collaborate with the murderer to be sure that Pogue could not arrive at the hospital in time to be saved. I am thinking about the accident on the bridge. The information I have is that the car that was stalled was a hired car. It was rented to an American woman, which is of interest to me. Her name is Rochelle C. Pierce. The rental agreement says that she is a travel agent. The name must be real because it would have been checked against a passport, but the profession is not necessarily true. I was wondering if the name means something to you or perhaps to your fiancé."

"Rochelle C. Pierce," said Celeste aloud. "No, I don't recognize the name." Turning to Mac she asked, "Do you know her?" He shook his head, puzzled. "The name doesn't mean anything to either of us," she informed Charron.

"Then we are still lost," sighed Charron. "I am sorry to disturb your weekend."

"No, it is I who contacted you," said Celeste. "I appreciate your attempt to help. I will continue to think about what you have told me. Perhaps something will make sense."

"Perhaps," said Charron. *"Au revoir et bon week-end."*

"Au revoir," said Celeste.

Celeste replaced the receiver and curled up under the duvet, facing away from Mac.

"Hey," protested Mac. "You've taken the quilt."

"Sorry," said Celeste, as she freed some duvet in

his direction, keeping her back to him. "It's a duvet, not a quilt."

"Okay, duvet. What'd he say?"

"Nothing helpful," said Celeste into her pillow.

"Celeste," commanded Mac. "Turn around and talk to me. You can't expect to solve these crimes in a day if they've stumped the Japanese and French police for weeks, not to mention the valiant law enforcement officers of Utah."

"I know, Mac, but things have got to be resolved or I'm unemployed. It's impossible not to think about it." Celeste rolled over, resuming a fetal position, but now facing him. Her short hair had twisted into a few wispy spikes that gave her a vulnerable, sleepy child look.

"Let me distract you," said Mac. "That's why I came to see you."

"Oh, Mac, is that all you can ever think about?" protested Celeste.

Mac answered wordlessly. He smoothed his hand over Celeste's forehead, causing her to shut her eyes. Then, he traced his finger from the center of her forehead down the long narrow bridge of her nose, over her lips, down her neck and between her breasts until he came to her knees drawn tightly into her stomach. Gently he pried the top knee apart from the bottom knee, as though opening a package, and, with a hand on either knee, urged Celeste to lie back on the bed by kissing her mouth.

The sensation of air between Celeste's open legs tickled deliciously. She willed her body to relax into oblivion. It was impossible not to surrender and wait luxuriously for Mac to descend.

• • •

It was almost noon by the time Celeste and Mac were ready to get out of bed, having fallen back asleep following the aftermath of Charron's phone call. Celeste continued to marvel at the intensity of sex with Mac. It blocked out everything else. She could hardly believe that this was going to be her privilege for the rest of her life.

Both agreed they were ravenous. They showered and dressed quickly, deciding to walk into Noe Valley to search for food. The weather was auspicious, in spite of the fact that it was close to the end of June. By July, when the heat of summer was established in the Central Valley, the fog would penetrate every evening and last through the morning, even into this more forgiving area of the city. Then, places like the BAU campus would be swamped for days on end with bone-chilling damp and gusty winds.

Today, the eclectic and lush gardens in front of the equally eclectic collection of houses in Celeste's neighborhood had been warming in the sun since early morning. In his professional gardening days, when Mac was finishing his undergraduate degree as a part-time student, he had planted many gardens in more salubrious neighborhoods of San Francisco. He had specialized in subtle, Japanese-style layouts with elegant, understated plants. While he enjoyed those projects and the botanical tranquillity they created, Mac always somewhat regretted that he couldn't take advantage of the profusion of flowering shrubs that survive in the San Francisco climate. This morning he delighted in the bursts of purple sage mixed with bright orange California poppies that decorated the

street with exuberance. He hadn't realized how much
he missed horticultural festivity in the tame community of Bethesda surrounding the National Institutes
of Health, where he now lived.

As if the flowers were not sufficiently exotic, a rau-
cous chorus of squawking accosted Mac and Celeste
as they were about to enter a local dim sum restaurant.
Flashes of brilliant yellow-green from a nearby tree
revealed that San Francisco's famous flock of feral
parrots was also out looking for brunch. This sighting
pleased Celeste tremendously. She always kept one
eye out for the parrots. They had been made legen-
dary in Armistead Maupin's *Tales of the City* and
their sporadic appearance added to the romantic feelings about San Francisco that Celeste had developed
since she moved out from the East Coast.

However, Celeste's sense of contentment lasted
only until the first steamed dumplings were served. A
silent waitress approached their table, pushing a cart
piled high with bamboo baskets. She lifted the cover
of one of the baskets for inspection of the contents.
In response to Mac's approval, the waitress placed the
uncovered basket on their table and used a self-inking
stamp to mark the card on the table to indicate what
she had served. The little dumplings were arranged
neatly in a group of four. Immediately Celeste was
reminded of the formal grouping of the snails served
in the restaurant on Noirmoutier. Food served in individual portions like dim sum or snails were the perfect vehicle for poisoning one diner without injuring
another.

Celeste tried to recall the layout of the restaurant
in Noirmoutier. The counter from which the waiters

collected the food destined for the dining room was open to the kitchen on one side and was accessed by the waiters from the other side through the cramped and rather dirty corridor that also led to the toilets for the restaurant guests. So everyone using the facilities had passed the waiting dishes. It wouldn't have been difficult to slip a dose of something into the extra snail. And it would have been obvious that the plate with the extra snail was earmarked for Pogue.

Access to the dishes being cleared from the head table had been more restricted. But, presumably, that was the moment when a poisoned shell would have been removed. The most remarkable thing that Celeste could remember about that moment was Wally Dyer's frantic command to the waiter to save the shells as they were cleared. In retrospect, this act seemed highly suspicious. Why would Dyer suggest testing the snails, if he hadn't known that one was poisoned? Removal of the evidence and then calling for a test would be a perfect strategy for diverting suspicion from the real cause of death.

"No," said Celeste out loud. "The motive is too far-fetched."

Mac had been watching Celeste as she went through these ruminations that were stimulated by the sight of the steamed dumplings. He had already eaten two dumplings while she sat there staring at the bamboo basket. "Ground control to Celeste," he said.

Celeste shook her head. "Sorry, Mac. I was just thinking about—"

"I know what you were thinking about. Who's your suspect now?"

"What would you say to Wally Dyer?"

"According to your criteria, he would have had to attend all three meetings," Mac pointed out. "He was at the ski meeting where Churchill died and he was at the French meeting, but he wasn't in Japan."

"If he worked with a collaborator, then only the collaborator would have had to be in Japan."

"True," said Mac. "What's the motive you were talking about?"

"I guess not dissimilar to the outrageous motive that Rank has provided for me," admitted Celeste.

"Meaning?"

"Well, Rank says that I have been killing off senior colleagues who might write negative letters regarding my promotion. I doubt that Dyer is yet being considered for tenure, but getting rid of the old guard would be one way for a young person to establish prominence in a field, although rather extreme. The only reason I thought of him was that he was so insistent on testing the snails, that he might have been confident that they were clean."

"I'll say it's extreme," agreed Mac. "But maybe there are other factors motivating Dyer that we don't know about. He's rather defensive about his relationship with Rank."

"Yeah, well, I gather that's just the age-old problem of the protégé and the sponsor being emotionally involved. No different from other lab-based romances. Like Janet Pogue and Richard, for that matter."

"I'm sure that Dyer doesn't intend to end up as completely eclipsed by Rank, as Janet was by Richard."

"It won't happen between two men. While it's socially more difficult for them as a couple, they have the professional advantage of separate names. And, there's no natural gender-biased assumption that one partner is inferior."

"Women don't have to take their husbands' names. I certainly won't expect you to, for example."

"But Janet and Richard were from an earlier generation, when it was expected. And besides, Janet's scientific career developed when she was already Mrs. Pogue. They married in college, even before enrolling for their doctoral degrees."

Celeste was suddenly and acutely visited by a strong sense of the familiar. She had confronted this topic of name change not that long ago. Celeste was once again absorbed in thought as Mac motioned for two servers in succession to unload additional plates of dim sum onto the table. An assortment of plates and baskets had been steadily expanding in front of them through this random process.

"You've got to eat some of this, Celeste," chided Mac.

"I will. It's just that I realized something potentially important," she replied with excitement. "When we were in Montana, Kirsten Larsen was goading Janet about establishing an independent identity and she said that it would be easier for Shelley Churchill because she already has a different professional name. Apparently she works for the family travel agency and for work purposes goes by her maiden name, which is the name of the business."

"So?"

"She's a travel agent, like Charron's mystery woman on the bridge. Rochelle C. Pierce."

"What's Shelley's maiden name?"

"I don't know, she never said. But Shelley could be a nickname for Rochelle."

"It could," said Mac, but he wasn't enthusiastic. "But what would her motivation be for killing Richard Pogue and Lars Larsen? Okay, I can understand wanting to kill George Churchill, especially if you were married to him. But—"

"If she teamed up with someone who wanted all three men dead for another reason, she might have helped so she could get rid of Churchill," interrupted Celeste.

"The motivation to get rid of Churchill would have to be pretty strong," said Mac. "Stronger than shacking up with some hunky ski guide. Though that affair was probably more a symptom of a bad relationship than a motive."

Celeste realized that Mac was referring to the fact that he had seen Shelley hanging around the staff lodge at the ski resort where Churchill was killed. "It could also have been accessory to murder," said Celeste, getting increasingly agitated. "Shelley could have distracted the guide while an accomplice tampered with Churchill's ski."

"Celeste," said Mac. "Eat. This is all ridiculous conjecture until you find out Shelley Churchill's maiden name. I'm not going to let it spoil our weekend together."

Celeste felt she now had a useful task she could set herself. With a focused question in mind, she calmed down sufficiently to finish the accumulated dim sum.

After lunch, Mac, in keeping with his vow to continue to enjoy the weekend, insisted that they take a walk before returning to Celeste's place. He fancied a nostalgic tour of the city and came up with the perfect excuse. He'd lived in and near San Francisco for his entire life, except for the years he spent in Vietnam and the last two years, when he had been completing his doctoral research at the National Institutes of Health. But he had never visited the San Francisco mission. He guessed they weren't far from the mission and suggested they walk down Dolores until they came to it.

Celeste agreed to a walk. She was feeling guilty about making Mac's visit worthwhile, although she hadn't, she reminded herself, invited him. Also she thought the mission wasn't that far away and that it wouldn't be long before she could be back home trying to solve the mystery of Shelley Churchill's maiden name. The most direct source of information would be Janet Pogue and she'd been planning to give Janet a ring anyway.

As it turned out, they were at least two miles from the mission. These were miles that were punctuated by several almost vertical ascents and descents from neighborhood to neighborhood. Celeste, who normally loved to explore the city on foot, became more and more impatient and increasingly irritable as the mission continued to elude them.

It was undoubtedly Celeste's irritability that led to the argument with Mac. It began when Celeste remarked on a building along Dolores where she had looked at a condominium for sale, before she had purchased her current unit. One thing led to another and she mentioned that she had just made the cutoff for the first round of bidding on Geoff and Maria's place.

Mac responded as though he had been betrayed. Celeste was not sympathetic. She, rather impatiently, tried to explain what she thought she had explained already, that the bid was simply to make sure she didn't lose the option of buying the unit. She asked Mac whether he was so convinced that she wasn't going to get tenure that he had ruled out the possibility of settling in San Francisco.

At least Mac understood the futility of arguing with a raw nerve. But he wondered to himself whether he would ever get Celeste to think as part of a couple. They continued along Dolores in a silence made solemn by the huge sentinels of palm trees that dominated that thoroughfare.

At last Celeste and Mac reached the mission. It glowed like a white confection against the blue sky. Also like a confection, it was teeming with little creatures. Children were milling around the entrance and the souvenir shop, antlike. They were comparing postcards and cheap plastic baubles, pinching, pulling, and teasing each other. The adults with them had given up on maintaining order and were gossiping among themselves alongside of the yellow school buses, which proclaimed that the group had come from San Juan Elementary School.

San Juan Bautista was the site of another one of the Spanish missions built before Californian statehood, and it was located a good hundred miles south of the city. If the group had come, as Celeste supposed, from one mission to another, she wasn't surprised that the children needed to let off steam. She also supposed that from that particular community, Saturday was the only day that a sufficient number of parents were off work to act as chaperones. Neither the behavior of the parents nor that of the children suggested that there was anything holy about this pilgrimage beyond an ordinary school trip. Nor had the exposure to the interior of the mission instilled any evident spirituality in the visitors. Celeste was profoundly depressed by the sight of these puffy, junk food–fed children and their commercial zeal over the souvenirs they had acquired.

Celeste, however, was susceptible to the charm of the mission, once inside. Raised Jewish, she was ecumenical about houses of worship and was uplifted by human monuments to spirituality, whether they were churches, cathedrals, mosques, or synagogues. A momentary peace descended and dispelled her irritation, as she and Mac wandered through the wooden basilica and inspected the stained glass windows depicting the other California missions. When they reached the intimate graveyard in the mission garden, Celeste took Mac's hand.

They wandered thus from headstone to headstone and Celeste was interested to read that most of the names on the gravestones were Irish. It occurred to Celeste that she knew shockingly little about the flux of different ethnic groups during the settlement of the city. She wondered what Mac was thinking about as he read these inscriptions. She realized, with some additional shock, that she also knew nothing about the ethnic or religious background of her future husband. It occurred to Celeste that a sensible person might have said they needed more time to get to know each other.

13

Shell Shock

Celeste awoke early Monday morning with an inspiration. She was thankful that there was no one to prevent her from getting out of bed to follow it up immediately. Mac had departed Sunday evening to stand by for the red-eye flight back to Washington.

Since Saturday, Celeste had been waiting for Janet Pogue to call her back, in response to the message she had left. But, if Mac hadn't been distracting her, Celeste would have probably thought sooner of going on the Web to find out what she needed to know. All she needed to do was to use a search engine to find a travel agency by the name of Pierce. If she was lucky, there might be photographs of the agents.

And Celeste was lucky. Pierce Travel, located in Concord, Massachusetts, had a group photograph of the "travel team" on its Web page. And there was Shelley Churchill, standing in the center of the group. The photograph had been taken before her recent haircut, but there was no mistaking her well-appointed figure and seductive attitude, not to mention her smug expression.

Celeste was elated at her discovery and then, as she considered the possible significance, horrified. This could mean that Shelley conspired with someone to tamper with her husband's ski while she kept the ski guide occupied. It could also mean that Shelley had collaborated with someone to kill Pogue by stalling a rented car on the bridge.

And, Celeste realized, Shelley had been on the boat when the Larsen accident happened. She had been part of the group with Kirsten and Janet when they all discussed with the dive master the significance of the name tags on the deep dive tanks.

However, Celeste reminded herself, the evidence against Shelley was all circumstantial. Also, at least two of the murders, if Pogue *was* murdered, depended on a mysterious collaborator. Furthermore, this collaborator would have to have a pressing motive to get rid of Pogue and Larsen, as well as Churchill. Celeste wondered if there was any connection between Shelley Churchill née Pierce and Wally Dyer or Ivan Rank or even Dot Grantham, for that matter. In any case, she should call Inspector Charron. Celeste went into her bedroom to find her wallet, where she had left Charron's business card.

Monday morning, Janet Pogue was also appreciating the solitude of living alone. It was now two months since Richard's death, two peaceful and restorative months. Janet had found infinitely many pleasurable aspects to life in the Bitterroot, once she was no longer a slave to producing culinary masterpieces at every meal. She took long walks down by the river and planted an extravagant flower garden where, in previous years, she had felt obliged to plant herbs and exotic vegetables. She was profoundly grateful to have finally achieved some harmony of spirit in her adult life, even if it would inevitably be cut short.

After a long, hot shower Janet stood dripping onto a new soft carpet on the slate floor of the bathroom, enjoying the warmth of the June sun penetrating the steam from the skylight above. She was thinking that as soon as she got dressed, she should phone Celeste Braun. After putting it off for a day, Janet knew that she couldn't postpone much longer. She plugged in the hair dryer and started to blow-dry her wet hair. Large clumps came freely away from her head as she applied her hairbrush. So, it had come as anticipated, the hair loss accompanying chemotherapy. A visit to the hat shop in San Francisco would have to be added to her schedule this week.

Janet was relieved that Celeste's message suggested that they meet for lunch when Janet was next in town. It would make it so much easier to resolve things. And now, though not for the best reason, Janet had a real excuse to be in San Francisco. Still, she had to solve the short-term problem of keeping Celeste quiet until they met. Janet wondered if she could temporarily get away with giving Celeste a false name. She doubted it. Celeste was too resourceful and might find another way to get Shelley's maiden name. Janet decided she'd have to develop an ad hoc strategy, once she spoke to Celeste. It could just be a coincidence that Celeste was interested in getting in touch with Shelley.

Janet's call connected just as Celeste reached out to pick up the receiver to phone Inspector Charron.

"Hi, Celeste, it's Janet Pogue," said Janet in response to Celeste's startled greeting.

"Oh, Janet, thanks for calling back. Just this morning I realized that I could use the Web to find Shelley's name. You're literally only minutes too late."

Good, thought Janet, on two accounts. First, she was glad she hadn't tried to give a false name. She couldn't have gotten away with it. Second, it sounded as though Celeste hadn't yet done anything with her information about Shelley. "I guess that's what's meant by being made obsolete by the Internet," Janet replied.

"Well, not completely obsolete. I can't have lunch with my computer. I'm also following up about the trip to San Francisco that you mentioned when I saw you in Japan. I was wondering if you're still planning to come down soon."

"As a matter of fact, I'll be there later in the week. My trip was just confirmed this morning. So, if you're free, we should have lunch. How does July first, Thursday, look for you?"

"July already," remarked Celeste. "This spring has gone so fast." As she checked her date book, it occurred to Celeste, belatedly, that the spring may not have gone so fast for Janet, who had suffered through her husband's death and the apparent return of her illness. "July first looks fine. Shall I make a reservation?".

"No, I'll take care of it. I've got connections at the Café Cormorant. An old friend is the manager. Shall we say noon?"

"That's great. I love their location, down in Fort Mason."

"Uh, Celeste," said Janet, "have you contacted Shelley yet?"

"No, not yet," said Celeste.

"You know, she's been very depressed recently, suicidal in fact. Evidently it's a delayed reaction to George's death. Maybe you should hold off getting in touch with her until I can tell you more on Thursday. Kirsten spoke to Shelley's doctor, who told her that Shelley was under treatment but not very stable."

"Oh," said Celeste with some surprise. Shelley Churchill had never seemed particularly delicate or sensitive. "Thanks for letting me know." She paused to evaluate the consequences of what Janet had just told her. "I guess what I have to say can wait a few days."

"Glad to hear it," said Janet. "You wouldn't want to precipitate a crisis without knowing the full story."

"Of course not," agreed Celeste.

"See you Thursday, then."

"I'll look forward to it."

Celeste felt the wind had been taken out of her sails. Under the circumstances, she now had a moral obligation to hold off from phoning Charron until she spoke further with Janet. But could she afford it, given the pressure on her to clear her own name from Rank's ridiculous accusation? Celeste had to face the fact that contacting Charron immediately might precipitate an unnecessary inquiry that would have serious consequences for Shelley's mental health. She had never particularly liked Shelley, but accusation for her husband's murder was not something done lightly. Though Charron seemed to be a sensible man, Celeste couldn't be sure how he would react to Celeste's identification of Shelley Churchill as Rochelle "Shelley" Pierce. He would almost certainly contact Shelley, so it would be better to find out exactly what her condition was.

It also occurred to Celeste, as she pondered her conversation with Janet, that there might very well be a legitimate explanation for Shelley's presence on the bridge the night that Richard died. It certainly wouldn't have been surprising if Shelley had been planning to join Kirsten and Janet for some touring after the conference, even if she hadn't been at the conference itself. Perhaps she would have arrived in time to make the final conference dinner, if her rented car hadn't stalled. Celeste knew she could easily get information about this from Janet on Thursday, when it would be natural to introduce the subject in the course of conversation. With considerable misgivings, Celeste resigned herself to wait. She fervently hoped that the Hidden Point deal, also scheduled for Thursday, would be resolved one way or the other before any taint of scandal at BAU, particularly one involving Celeste, could jeopardize it.

Breaking into her turbulent thoughts, the telephone startled Celeste for the second time that morning.

It was Karen Klein, phoning from the lab. A fax had just come through from the journal to which they had submitted Karen's manuscript. The journal, Karen told Celeste, was happy to accept the manuscript, with essentially no revisions to be made. In addition, they wanted to expedite the publication date in order to coordinate with the publication of Rank's manuscript so that a commentary piece could be published at the same time.

A surge of relief and exaltation suffused Celeste's entire being. The world of scientific publishing could be brutally arbitrary. But the acceptance of a manuscript made one feel part of a glorious enterprise. And so much had been at stake with this manuscript. Now, so much would be set right. Celeste could sense Karen's corresponding pride, as she congratulated her, and wanted to see her face, to share their triumph. She told Karen she would be at the lab shortly, as soon as she picked up a bottle of champagne.

There were no champagne corks popping in Ivan Rank's department. It was ominously quiet as Wally Dyer proceeded down the corridor toward his office. The corridor was lined with enlarged images of virus particles, photographed through an electron microscope. The micrographs, as they were called, were framed and matted, as though being exhibited in an art gallery, but the overall impression was that the corridor was infested with virus. Wally stopped to inspect some of the images. Though he had passed the pictures every day for almost two years, he had paid them little attention. This morning, he needed an outlet for his preoccupation.

The phone call on Saturday, from the French police inspector, he had found only mildly annoying. In fact, he had already realized that he might be able to use it to his advantage. He was far more concerned about what was going to happen in his department.

At last Wally tired of the pictures and approached his office door. He unlocked it, let himself in, and relocked the door behind him. Inside, he hesitated for a moment. Then he sat down at his desk and picked up the telephone.

The phone rang at the other end and Dot Grantham's secretary put him through.

"Wally," said Grantham. "I thought I might hear from you sooner or later. I hope you have some good news for me."

"Good and bad," said Wally. "I've just come from the hospital. Ivan's not well. I'm very worried about him. He may have to retire."

"What's happened?"

"Well, I really shouldn't say too much, but I'm sure you would want to know the situation. Ivan's nerves have never been very strong and we've just had some news that seriously upset him. It has to do with a member of your faculty who's been dogging our research."

"Yes, I'm well aware of that situation," said Grantham. "She hasn't scooped you, I hope."

"Oh, no, nothing like that. But she's pushed her way into what should be exclusively our limelight."

"This is intolerable," said Grantham. "We can't be promoting junior faculty who have no scruples."

"I doubt she would see it that way," said Wally.

"Well, that's the problem, isn't it."

"I suppose you're right. In fact, I think she's been trying to divert suspicion from herself, regarding the, uh, terrible tragedies in our field. I just got a call from the French police this weekend. It's highly insulting."

"That's dreadful, dear." Dot Grantham was hardly a person to use terms of affection for her colleagues, but Wally Dyer was such a wholesome young man that he seemed to invite them.

"Anyway, I think you know why I'm calling," said Wally. "With Ivan out of commission, things are going to change here and I'm not sure it will be for the better."

"It sounds like it might be time for us to invite you to give a seminar to our faculty."

"Why, thanks," said Wally. "I was thinking the same thing. I heard that you were looking to expand in the area of virology and I have some interesting ideas I could share with you."

"How soon can you come out? We're about to finalize the plans for the move to Hidden Point, which will initiate a lot of discussion about new facilities on both campuses."

"Next week would work. It's easier to travel while Ivan's still in the hospital."

"Wonderful. I'll check which of the seminar times are free and get back to you. Most of the seminar series don't have regularly scheduled speakers after the end of June and it would be good if we could take advantage of one of the scheduled seminar times. I'd like to make sure there's a reasonable crowd to hear what you have to say. And, I'm sure I don't need to emphasize that it will be important for you to distinguish your work from that of our own faculty and make it clear how relatively important your own contributions are."

"Thanks for the advice," said Wally. "I'll book the trip as soon as I hear from you."

Grantham replaced the receiver and allowed herself to gloat a bit before she started making the necessary inquiries to finalize arrangements for Wally Dyer's visit. With Rank practically out of the picture and the

recent deaths of the senior virologists, Wally Dyer
was looking like he would be one of the dominant
investigators in the field of molecular virology. It
would be quite a coup to attract him to her department. If he discredited Celeste Braun in the process,
Grantham would be free to make a strong offer to
Russo, as well. There was, of course, also the far-
fetched possibility that Celeste might be arrested for
murder. Although Grantham didn't believe Rank's accusation, there was nothing to be gained by dismiss-
ing it entirely. And, no matter what the truth was,
being accused of murder did not say much for the
reputation of Celeste Braun's character. Grantham realized, with anticipatory satisfaction, that her months
of planning and scheming were now about to come
to fruition.

14

Out to Lunch

The dawning of July first, being a Thursday, was heralded by the noise of the weekly garbage collection for Celeste's neighborhood. Unable to get back to sleep, Celeste turned off the alarm and got up to make herself breakfast. Walking out into the living room, she saw, through the picture windows, that the fog had crept in the night before. Celeste's splendid view of the city was now arranged against a background of dull gray, as it would be until September.

The view made Celeste all too aware that today was the day that the second bids on Geoff and Maria's condominium had to be made. The bids were due at the real estate office by five P.M. There had been eighteen bidders in the first round, but the real estate agent had told Celeste, confidentially, that she expected at least five to drop out. She had also told Celeste how much she would have to bid to be in the running to get the property. Privately, Celeste wondered how many people were given these apparently privileged pieces of information. With the real estate agents in control of bidding wars, it was no surprise that the prices of San Francisco real estate were rising exponentially. Nonetheless, Celeste had spent a good part of the past two days on the telephone, trying to mobilize her finances. Whether or not she would actually go through with making the bid, the preparation was a welcome distraction from all the other concerns that were nagging her.

After the first day of looking into the policy of borrowing from her retirement savings and the possibility of taking out a second mortgage, Celeste thought she wasn't even going to come close to what she needed. Then yesterday morning she got the idea of involving her brother. He had been living abroad since he graduated from business school, mostly commuting between Saudi Arabia and South Africa. Celeste knew that he had been accumulating obscene sums of money for his work as an investment consultant. She proposed to him that he might want to coinvest in her property, as a way of getting into the home real estate market. He actually thanked her for the opportunity, which gave Celeste both confidence about the investment and an excuse to proceed. The excuse of course would be badly needed to explain herself to Mac, if she did proceed.

Retreating into the kitchen, Celeste turned on the radio and then filled the kettle to make tea. Bob Edwards announcing the *Morning Edition* program for National Public Radio remained the most constant male presence in the mornings of Celeste's adult life. She would never become disenchanted with his deep and reassuring voice but lately she noticed that the segments in between the news broadcasts had become increasingly banal and poorly edited. No doubt it was a function of the perpetually decreasing congressional support for public broadcasting.

Celeste cut up a banana onto a bowl of bran flakes and suffered through a whining and sentimental opinion piece on how cyberdogs could never replace man's best friend. This was followed by a politically correct and overlong story about the power of advertising in influencing teenagers either to start or not to start smoking. Celeste was considering turning off the radio, for the ten minutes remaining before the hourly news, when the California report began.

The lead story was about the failure of Bay Area University to make the city's deadline for a financial commitment to develop an extension of the campus at Hidden Point. The provost was given a spot for comment.

"Naturally, we are tremendously disappointed," Celeste heard his familiar voice say. "This will certainly mean some regrouping at our present site and rethinking our plans for expansion. Nonetheless, our goal is to continue to serve the city of San Francisco as a world-class medical center and we will persist in realizing that goal." The next spot was the spokesperson for the Hidden Point community, who declared it a triumph for the neighborhood, that it would not be exploited by unchecked development.

Celeste's heart leapt. The shit would hit the fan. But when it settled, the BAU that Celeste knew and loved would be intact.

Celeste was not surprised that, within fifteen minutes of her arrival at work, she received a summons to Dot Grantham's office. Celeste knew that Grantham couldn't possibly fare well in the aftermath of the failure of Hidden Point. But Grantham could still do a lot of damage to Celeste's career at BAU, even if Grantham herself would not benefit from the consequences.

This morning, Celeste noted with interest, Grantham was wearing a suit in an unbecoming shade of salmon pink, with ghastly lipstick to match. She appeared to be putting on a cheerful front in the face of what must be great personal setback.

"I won't beat about the bush, Celeste," began Grantham. "Officially, as of today, I am returning to the Department of Medicine, as vice-chair. Dr. Rosenthal has agreed to come out of retirement and serve as acting chair for Micro until a replacement is found. Because of the problems in getting letters of support for you this year, your tenure review will be delayed until the fall quarter."

"I don't know what to say," responded Celeste. She knew she should protest that her academic clock was being slowed. But she was enormously relieved that Grantham was no longer responsible for her promotion, not to mention that Dr. Rosenthal, who hired Celeste in the first place, might be.

"If I were you, I'd keep a low profile and not say anything," warned Grantham. "You're lucky that the Hidden Point financing failed before there was any scandal with your name associated with it. But you should be aware that Wally Dyer is giving a talk on campus next week. Then your whole sordid story will come out and I doubt there will be much left of your reputation for even Rosenthal to save."

Celeste wondered what had transpired between

Grantham and Dyer. She replied, "Dyer's work is complementary to ours. There's not much of a sordid story there."

"*Complementary* is a subjective term," said Grantham. "Now, if you'll excuse me, there are other department members I need to see."

Celeste couldn't resist saying as she left, "Thanks for letting me know where things stand, Dot. I guess this means I'm off the Hidden Point planning committee."

Dot Grantham's pink lips were set grimly as she glared at Celeste's jean-clad backside. She found the fact that Celeste persisted in wearing jeans almost as annoying as the rudeness of her parting remark. But Dot Grantham was confident of having the last word. The department might not be expanding under her leadership anymore, or even expanding much at all, but if Celeste did not get tenure, it would still open up a place for Wally Dyer, if he were looking to leave Rank's nest.

The Café Cormorant was located on a pier at Fort Mason. The side of the restaurant facing the bay was entirely glass, affording a view of the marina and, in the distance, the Golden Gate Bridge. Celeste had the sensation of stepping out on the water whenever she entered the restaurant. The sun hadn't managed to filter through this first serious summer fog, so the colors of the moored boats and the bridge took on a deep, rich hue in contrast to the gray of the water and sky.

Celeste was about to speak to the hostess, when she saw Janet Pogue waving to her from a table near the window.

"I see them," said Celeste. "You don't have to seat me." And indeed, she saw them. To Celeste's surprise, Janet was accompanied by Kirsten and Shelley. The shadow cabinet was assembled in full.

What Celeste next experienced could only be described as a revelation in cinematic slow motion. She stepped down from the foyer deck into the dining area and watched the three women as she approached them. Janet was holding court. Shelley appeared healthy and happy and was laughing at something Janet was saying. Kirsten was listening with a smile on her face and was toying with the utensils in front of her.

It was Kirsten's idle gestures that jogged Celeste's memory. Kirsten had been toying with the snail shells on Richard Pogue's plate, just before the plate was cleared away. It was undoubtedly, then, she who had pocketed the snail. Shelley had purposely stalled the car on the bridge to block traffic to the hospital. Janet had left the table to use the toilet during Richard's harangue, and could have doctored the snail. She would certainly have had access to many effective poisons from the laboratory. Shelley had slept with the ski guide to keep him from the lockers. Kirsten had been on the heli-ski trip and therefore had access to the lockers early in the morning. Janet had pleaded seasickness on the dive trip. All three wives had remained on deck during the dive briefings and had plenty of opportunity to switch the tank tags. The shared bond of unendurable husbands and marital traps had united them. They had, with ultimate vengeance, engineered their own liberation. Celeste had to ask herself whether she had the heart or the courage to spoil their plan.

Celeste reached the table and found she couldn't open her mouth. She stood looking from woman to woman, searching their faces to see if she had understood the truth.

"Why don't you sit down, Celeste?" invited Janet. "I have something to tell you."

Celeste started to greet them, when Janet held up her hand. "I think it's probably best if you let me talk first. You wouldn't want to say anything you'd regret." Celeste obediently sat down in the chair, which Kirsten had pulled out for her.

"I'm here on a hat-buying trip," said Janet. Her tone was matter-of-fact. "I've done it before, as you know. Last time the remission lasted fifteen years. This time, the prognosis is not so rosy. But there is nothing wrong with Kirsten and Shelley. They have many free and happy years ahead of them. So, I apologize for the little fib I had to tell you about Shelley's condition. Now, we need to get the rest of the facts straight. But first, we'd appreciate it if you could answer one question."

"Sure," said Celeste. Her mouth was dry. She took a sip from the water glass in front of her. It was sweating and had a slice of lemon floating in it.

"To whom are you planning to give the information regarding Shelley's professional name?"

"Inspector Charron."

"Good, that's what we thought. We wanted to make sure that you knew that Shelley had been on her way to meet us at the dinner the night that Richard died. She was joining us for a trip around Brittany following the conference and I was expecting her to be on the bridge. I'm also a pretty good car mechanic. Shelley recalls that she left the rented car unattended that afternoon. Kirsten will verify that after we bought the snails, I went off by myself. In fact, I was late meeting her at the hotel. I'm sure you'll remember that we only just made the bus."

"I remember," agreed Celeste.

"Anything else you'd like to know?" asked Janet.

Celeste thought she comprehended what Janet was saying. It seemed Janet intended to take the blame as the single perpetrator of the murder in France. And, she certainly could have switched the tank tags on the diving trip. Was it possible that Janet intended to take the rap for all three murders, Celeste wondered.

"You weren't at the ski meeting, were you? You can't take responsibility for that," Celeste pointed out.

"No, I wasn't at the meeting, but it's only an eight hour drive to Salt Lake City from where I live in Montana. That's why there will be no flight records. Kirsten and Shelley will confirm that I drove down to meet them for a spa vacation after the ski meeting. I knew about Shelley's affair with the ski instructor. I also knew that the heli-ski trip was planned during the day that I was supposed to arrive. It was easy to drive down a day early." The two other women nodded their heads in verification.

"As for a motive, though," said Celeste slowly, "it's easier to believe that all three of you collaborated."

"For you, perhaps," replied Janet. "But what does the male world know about what motivates women? They'll sooner understand a misguided vendetta against husband-scientists by an embittered wife than an organized campaign for revenge and emancipation."

"You didn't plan for it to end this way," remarked Celeste.

"No, but I didn't plan on a relapse either. Nor did we plan on your involvement in investigating what happened, which perhaps you would be so kind as to explain."

Celeste did explain. She described how Ivan Rank and Dot Grantham had, through jealousy and greed, jointly ruined the wives' plan by accusing Celeste of the murders.

"Oh, dear," said Janet, with genuine concern. "We never dreamed that this might jeopardize your tenure promotion."

"I don't think you really made the situation any worse than it would have been anyway," said Celeste. "They would have found another way to create trouble for me."

"That's generous of you, dear," said Janet. "Now, shall we order lunch?"

After lunch, Celeste left the restaurant with permission to phone Charron, as she had originally intended to do. She knew that the case would be resolved as the women had planned. Their stories and alibis were watertight and there was nothing Celeste could say that would be an effective challenge, even if she knew the truth were otherwise. And what would be the point?

Celeste thought she could accept the situation, but she needed to sort through it all again, before being

sure. The confrontation in the restaurant had left her
somewhat dumbfounded, to say the least. She turned
in the opposite direction from where her car was
parked and walked along the driveway from which
the Fort Mason piers projected into the water. The
driveway ended abruptly at a seawall, with a rickety
wooden staircase leading up to the city park above
Fort Mason.

Celeste recalled that there was a bayside walking
trail that extended from the park down onto the next
pier. She toiled up the stairs to join the path and
turned left at the top to descend back toward the bay.
Slightly breathless from the climb, Celeste proceeded
down the path. She was flanked on her right by a
sheltered tunnel of cypress trees and on her left was
the view of the bay and the Golden Gate. While Celeste walked, she tried to organize her thoughts.

Celeste was absolutely convinced that all three
women had been involved in planning and effecting
the murders of their husbands. With Janet taking all
the blame, two murderers would go free. And Celeste
was impotent to do anything about it. She had no
choice but to come to terms with being rendered in-
effectual. Celeste was grateful that, at least, she had
the certain knowledge that these were not individuals
who would murder again. Celeste also realized, with
an ironic sense of consolation, that, from their perspective, all three women had already served their
prison terms.

And it was this latter thought that was perhaps the
most disturbing. The sentences of these three intelligent and capable women had been decreed on the
marriage altar. Not only had they sacrificed their per-

sonal potential to that of their husbands, but their
servicing of their husbands had empowered the men
to become ruthless careerists. And, in addition to the
wives, the children of all three marriages were casu-
alties. From her acquaintance with the shadow cabinet, Celeste was painfully aware that the Churchill,
Pogue, and Larsen offspring were a sorry group of
delinquents, idlers, and drop-outs. Celeste could at
least fathom why these women did not consider di-
vorce as sufficient retribution for their destructive ser-
vitude, even if she could not condone the extremity
of their retaliation. Intellectually, Celeste knew that
marriage to Mac would be different. The climate
change in social expectations, as well as her scientific
seniority, would automatically dictate a different kind
of relationship. But did two careerists make a marriage any better? And, if Mac did manage to persuade
her to have a child, would they have any time for
each other? Celeste didn't think she could avoid
having her plans of marriage with Mac tainted by the
thought of what these women had done to escape
theirs.

Celeste reached the junction of the next pier with
the bay shore. This pier was a sturdy cement structure,
originally built for docking large ships. It was dotted
by fishermen, standing along each side. Celeste
walked between them, toward the tip of the pier. The
fishermen faced the water, watching their lines. By
the set of their nylon-jacketed backs, Celeste could
sense their chill. It was not a surprising state, given
the steadily gusting wind blowing in from the ocean.
Each fisherman was accompanied by a woman wearing a similar nylon jacket, sitting glumly in a portable

deck chair, with her back to the water and to the fisherman she was with. Hugging themselves against the wind, the women were silently engaged in watching their children at play in the center of the pier. It was as though the scene before her had been staged as a theatrical negation of the modernized partnership that Celeste had envisaged for herself and Mac. These miserable couples defiantly represented the timeless roles of male provider and female caretaker and the lack of communication between them. They seemed to embody the explanation for the shadow cabinet taking justice into their own hands.

Celeste reached the end of the pier and looked out over the water, with her back turned on this domestic stage. She focused on the effortless coordination between five pelicans, who glided in front of her in single file, suspended only a few feet above the water's surface. These birds, like the feral parrots, epitomized aspects of San Francisco that made Celeste want to call it home. Growing up in the Northeast, the pelican was familiar to Celeste only as a storybook bird, and it thrilled her to think that she now actually lived in a place where pelicans lived too.

Celeste had to admit to herself that if her tenure at BAU were granted and she could stay in San Francisco, she would choose to. And if she accepted this self-confession, then she should take the plunge and bid on the rest of the property where she eventually hoped to settle. Property could always be sold, if things didn't work out, but the option of buying it would not wait.

Of course, the option of Mac might not wait either. And it was unlikely that they would marry now, if she took this step. It wasn't that Celeste didn't love him and wouldn't still. God knows she had never loved anyone so intensely. But there were so many things each had to resolve individually, it was the wrong time to tie together their fates. And if being with Mac turned out to be the right option, it would come around again. Maybe then circumstances would be more auspicious.

Celeste turned and walked back down the pier toward the shore, her car, and her next destination, the office of her real estate agent. She felt hollow and sad, as the wind penetrated her tweed jacket, but, at the same time, it was an energizing, liberating wind.

EPILOGUE

The headline of the *New York Times* article reporting the breakthrough on the bioblaster murders was CHER-CHEZ LA FEMME. The article included an impressive photograph of Inspector Charron, with his pipe clenched between his teeth. Celeste felt a twinge of nostalgia as she recalled that Mac had teased her with the same French expression. Ironically, Mac's joke had predicted the truth.

Celeste wouldn't know how Mac had reacted to the article or whether he had even seen it. He had frostily terminated their engagement when she told him about making her real estate bid. He didn't even know that Celeste was now the owner of her entire building.

But Celeste had more immediate worries on her mind the morning the story about Janet Pogue was released. In fact, she had been reading the paper over coffee, in her neighborhood bakery, postponing her departure for work. She was not anxious to confront the reality that Wally Dyer's seminar at BAU was scheduled for noon that day.

Finally, at about ten A.M., Celeste joined the crowd

of people waiting at the elevators to the BAU laboratory towers. She couldn't help but wonder whom Dyer would be meeting with that morning and whether she would have to confront hostility from colleagues even before his seminar.

It wasn't until Celeste got to her office and checked her e-mail that she learned that Wally Dyer's lecture had been canceled. Hardly believing her luck, she rushed out to the department office and checked the seminar notice board. Indeed, across the flyer announcing Dyer's lecture the word *canceled* had been scrawled in red marker pen.

So Celeste's private suspicion was confirmed. Dyer had only been interested in Grantham's offer if it included the resources that would have been available had the Hidden Point project succeeded. Thanks to his greed, Celeste's reputation would remain intact. And, when the manuscripts from both laboratories were published, the work and the commentary would speak for itself. Then her colleagues could make up their own minds about the value of her contributions.

Two hours later, Celeste was lying on the floor in the gymnasium across the street from the building where her laboratory was located. Finding herself blessedly free at noon, she attended one of the midday yoga classes. The yoga class participants included a few faculty and students and a fair number of the administrative staff of the medical center, as well as outsiders, who were welcome to join the campus fitness facility. These classes were considered a temporary refuge by those who attended and they all held them to be sacred, undoubtedly due to the influence of their extraordinary teacher. Seema herself was a part-time office administrative assistant on campus and her familiarity with the stress of BAU made her a particularly sympathetic instructor. Although the class participants were ostensibly registered for assigned sessions, Seema was relaxed about the schedule and welcomed any of her regular students at any time. This was a tremendous boon to Celeste, who often missed her scheduled class when she was out of town. And there was nothing like trying to twist your body into an impossible posture to free the mind.

Sure enough, as Celeste adopted the fish position and looked at the gymnasium upside down, she realized that there was still one unresolved loose end in the series of issues that had been plaguing her during this remarkable year. And, wonderfully, it was something she would be able to mend.

With this realization, Celeste sat bolt upright, much to the astonishment of her teacher. Celeste was thinking of her unwavering friend, Harry Freeman. Perhaps she thought of him because she had been reading his newspaper earlier in the day. She hadn't yet told him about her successful bid on the property. Once he knew the circumstances, he would insist on visiting San Francisco to celebrate.

From the *New York Times* bestselling author of *An Instance of the Fingerpost*

IAIN PEARS

Death and Restoration
__0-425-17742-4/$6.50

The Titian Committee
__0-425-16895-6/$6.50

The Last Judgement
__0-425-17148-5/$6.50

The Raphael Affair
__0-425-16613-9/$6.50

Giotto's Hand
__0-425-17358-5/$6.50

"Elegant...a piece of structural engineering any artist would envy."—*The New York Times*